Dinah in Love

Dinah in Love

Claudia Mills

Macmillan Publishing Company
New York

Maxwell Macmillan Canada
Toronto

Maxwell Macmillan International
New York   Oxford   Singapore   Sydney

Macmillan Publishing Company is part of the Maxwell Communication Group
of Companies.
Macmillan Publishing Company
866 Third Avenue
New York, NY 10022
Maxwell Macmillan Canada, Inc.
1200 Eglinton Avenue East
Suite 200
Don Mills, Ontario M3C 3N1
First edition
Printed in the United States of America

10 9 8 7 6 5 4 3 2 1

The text of this book is set in 12 point Sabon.

Mills, Claudia.
Dinah in love / Claudia Mills. — 1st ed.
p.   cm.
Summary: Dynamite Dinah finds her feelings about sixth-grade
classmate Nick Tribble changing when they share involvement in a
school play, a debate, and a sock hop.
ISBN 0-02-766998-X
[1. Schools—Fiction. 2. Interpersonal relations—Fiction.]
I. Title.
PZ7.M63963Dk   1993
[Fic]—dc20   93-19258

For R. E. T.,
with whom I once debated capital punishment

1

The socks were orange. Not the ordinary orange of carrots or pumpkins or marigolds in summer bloom, but a shocking, shrieking neon orange—the color socks might turn if they had been left behind during the core meltdown of a nuclear power plant. WE GLOW IN THE DARK! it said on the label. THEY'LL BE SURE TO SEE YOU WHEN YOU WEAR NIGHT-GLO SOXS FROM THE SOX COMPANY!

Dinah Seabrooke wiggled her toes with pleasure. "I'll take these," she told her father. "The orange ones, and the pink ones, too. I'll wear orange on one foot, pink on the other."

The pink socks were, if anything, even more electrifying than the orange socks. Looking at them made Dinah's eyes twitch.

"When these came into the store, I wondered who on earth would buy them," Dinah's father said. "Now I know."

Dinah's father was the manager of a sporting goods store. The socks were meant for joggers and cyclists who would be out exercising at night. Motorists would certainly notice them. Dinah had no intention of exercising at night. She needed socks that everyone would notice because she was the publicity chairperson of the sixth-grade sock hop at John F. Kennedy Middle School. And, besides, Dinah liked to be noticed. It made her feel alive in a special, tingling-all-over way.

Hey, did you see those socks! she imagined one sixth grader saying to another, as she dashed by in a blur of blinding pink and orange. Who was that wearing them?

Dinah Seabrooke, the other would answer. And in the same breath, both would exclaim, Of course!

But this time Dinah wanted to be noticed for a purely noble, unselfish reason. The purpose of the sock hop was to raise money for the recycling program at Dinah's school. So even though a sock hop was a dance where girls were going to dance with boys, Dinah wanted every sixth grader to go. If wearing the loudest, brightest, most noticeable socks in Riverdale would help a good cause, Dinah was willing to do her part.

Dinah herself was not going to dance with any boys, however. Dinah wasn't the type to dance with boys. She was the type to dance alone, on the school roof, in the rain, with everyone else looking out the window at her in awestruck amazement. She had actually done that once, back when she was in fifth grade, and of all her life so far it was her favorite memory.

Dinah peeled off the orange socks and handed both pairs to her father. She followed him over to the cash register and perched on the counter next to him as he rang them up.

"Have you decided yet who you're inviting to the dance?" Dinah's father asked her with a mischievous chuckle.

Dinah made a face. Blaine Yarborough, the sixth-grade class president, had announced that the sock hop would be a "Sadie Hawkins" dance, where girls asked boys, though of course kids could also go to the dance alone.

"I'll ask Benjamin," Dinah said. Benjamin was Dinah's baby brother, who had just turned one a month ago, at the beginning of March.

"Hmm." Dinah's father looked thoughtful. "He can walk, and he has six teeth. But he's not much of a conversationalist. Or a dancer, either, though I suppose in the next few weeks we could teach him a passable fox-trot."

"Oh, Daddy," Dinah said. "I'm going to go to the dance, since I sort of have to, but I'm not going to *dance*."

"Famous last words," her father said. "Look, honey, Saturdays start to get busy in here around this time. Why don't you settle down in back with a book, unless you want to help out for a while."

"I'll help," Dinah said promptly. "Can I change the clothes on the mannequin in the window?"

Dinah could tell that wasn't the kind of help he had in mind. He probably wanted her to do something useful, like straighten the lingerie table, where the leotards, tights, and exercise bras were all in a jumble. But her father only sighed and said, "Be my guest."

Dinah was already pouncing on the sale table, gathering up various items that might come in handy. She loved rearranging the display window that looked out on Riverdale's busy main street, although her father usually rearranged her rearranging as soon as he could. Today the mannequin, dressed in khaki pants, flannel shirt, and hiking boots, sat next to a tent, tending a fake camp fire. For a start, Dinah replaced the boots with scuba-diving flippers. Out in the street a middle-aged couple stopped to watch, and so did a couple of high-school kids. They laughed when Dinah exchanged the mannequin's denim sun hat for a shiny yellow football helmet. The passersby were joined by a family with redheaded twins in a double stroller and a woman writing parking tickets. Dinah slipped a baseball glove onto the mannequin's right hand.

After a few more changes like these, the high-school kids and the ticket woman drifted away. Dinah needed to think of something else.

She had it! *She* would be the mannequin.

Awkwardly, Dinah dragged the store mannequin out of the window and propped it up against a wall, out of sight from the street. Then she scrambled back up to take its place. Everything she was wearing—pants, T-shirt, and sneakers—had come from her father's store, so she looked the part. She knelt by the camp fire and pretended to light a match. Then, her hand upraised in midmotion, she froze into absolute stillness, hardly daring to breathe lest she spoil the effect.

It took her audience a minute or two to figure out what she was doing. Then she heard more laughter. Dinah didn't react. The crowd outside the window grew. One little boy kept shouting, "Is she real, Mommy? Mommy? Is she real or pretend? Mommy? Is she?"

Maybe Dinah had a future as the Living Mannequin. All the world's most famous department stores would beg her to come stand in their windows for a thousand dollars an hour. But being a living mannequin was hard work. Dinah would never have guessed that it was so difficult to do nothing, nothing at all, for whole minutes in a row. How did artists' models hold their poses for the days and weeks and months it took the artists to paint them? Maybe Mona Lisa had a mysterious smile because she was trying with all her might not to blink or sneeze or scratch her nose.

Being a living mannequin, it was turning out, was also boring. Dinah began to wish that she had made herself into a windup doll instead. She could have tended the fire and crawled in and out of the tent with little jerky doll motions. But it was too late for that now. A living mannequin she was, and a living mannequin she had to stay.

Out of the corner of her eye Dinah saw two newcomers to the crowd, a tall boy Dinah's age and a man who looked like he might be the boy's father. Dinah knew the boy slightly from school. His name was Nick Tribble. Nick's family had moved to Riverdale a few weeks ago, and he was in several of Dinah's classes, but Dinah couldn't remember that they had ever spoken. The other girls thought he was good-looking. He was already popular with the boys, like Artie Adams and Jason Winfield.

Dinah's hand—the one that held the match—began to ache. She willed it not to tremble. You are the world-famous Living Mannequin, she told herself, the Girl Who Never Moves!

Someone was pounding on the window. Dinah knew without looking that it had to be Nick.

"Hey, Dinah. Oh, Di-nah!" Dinah heard him call through the glass. "I bet I can get you to move, Dinah Ocean-River."

Fat chance. Dinah held her pose even more rigidly than before. Maybe that was how Mona Lisa had done it. Maybe Leonardo da Vinci had hired boys from her school to bet they could make her crack up.

"Oh, Mediterranean! Oh, Baltic!"

Dinah refused to laugh. She had heard jokes about her name before.

Nick pressed his face against the glass, so that his nose was squashed flat and his lips were long and rubbery, like a monstrous Halloween mask.

Dinah ignored him. Finally, Nick disappeared from view. Victory for Dinah! But no. Nick and his father had come into the store, and Nick stood grinning at Dinah from the rear of the window, where she had forgotten to pull the sliding screen shut behind her.

"Hey, Dinah! Long time no see . . . brook."

It was harder to ignore Nick now that there was no protective glass between them. But Dinah did her best. You are the world-famous Living Mannequin. You are the world-famous Living Mannequin. She imagined a crowd of several thousand pressing forward on tiptoe to catch a glimpse of her, the Girl Who Never—

Something landed on Dinah's head, something soft and clinging. Outside the window, the crowd of several thousand broke into loud laughter. Obviously Nick had thrown something at her, something extremely comical. But what?

A pink elastic strap fell across Dinah's left eye. Suddenly Dinah knew what it was that Nick had tossed her way. Dangling from the head of the world-famous Living Mannequin was a Just-for-Her Extra-Support Exercise Bra.

The Living Mannequin had had enough, more than enough, from Mr. Nick Tribble. Dinah tore the bra off her head and leaped down from the window in furious pursuit of Nick, who had wisely set off at a run. Bra in hand, she chased him twice around her father's store. She would kill him when she caught him. He would be the first boy in history strangled with a $14.99 Just-for-Her brassiere.

"Dinah! What on earth is going on here?" The voice was her father's.

"Nick! Stop that running. Stop it, I tell you." This from Mr. Tribble.

Nick dashed out the front door of the store. Dinah pelted after him. But Nick was too fast for her. Dinah never would have overtaken him if a delivery van hadn't conveniently backed out of the alley behind Griffith's Hardware, blocking Nick's path.

Nick turned around to face her. "I won," he crowed. "You moved."

Dinah lunged at him with her lethal pink weapon. Nick caught her wrists and stood grinning down at her, as she struggled to free herself from his grip and proceed with the murder.

"Don't be mad," he said. "You have to admit it was pretty funny."

"I do not," Dinah said. But she stopped fighting. Nick let go of her hands, and she whirled on her heel and marched back to the store. Nick followed her, still laughing.

Dinah knew her father would be angry at her for causing a disturbance in the store. But it had been all Nick's fault, every last bit of it. She hated Nick as she had never hated another boy, even Artie and Jason, who, for all their teasing, had never thrown a bra at her in front of a horde of her fans.

Back at the store, Dinah went to collect her scolding, and Nick his.

"Just remember this, Ocean-River," Nick called after her. "I said I'd make you move, and I did."

I hate you, Nick Tribble, Dinah thought. I hate the very marrow of your moldy bones! And yet—the strong emotion that overcame her didn't feel like hatred, exactly. It felt like—it just felt different, somehow, in a way Dinah couldn't quite describe.

2

"He likes you."

Dinah stared at her best friend, Suzanne Kelly, in disbelief. "He *what*?!"

"He likes you," Suzanne repeated matter-of-factly. "A boy doesn't throw a bra at a girl unless he likes her."

Dinah flung back the covers of her bed. It was Saturday night, and she was sleeping over at Suzanne's house. "He does not like me. Greg Thomas likes *you*. Has he ever thrown a bra at you?"

"I didn't say *all* boys throw bras at girls they like. I said a boy wouldn't throw a bra at a girl *unless* he liked her."

"That is the most ridiculous thing I ever heard," Dinah protested. But Suzanne's calm authority made everything she said, however ridiculous, sound right and reasonable. And over the course of sixth grade, Suzanne had become something of an expert on boys. She even had a real-live boyfriend, who passed notes to her in public and called her on the telephone. Of course, Greg was as much a friend as he was a boyfriend.

"Ask him to the sock hop," Suzanne said.

This time Dinah threw a pillow at her. "I wouldn't ask Nick Tribble to a dance if my life depended on it. I told Blaine right from the start that a Sadie Hawkins dance was a dumb idea and I wasn't going to ask anybody."

"You'd better do it soon," Suzanne advised. "I think Katie Richards likes him, too."

"Likes him, *too?*" Dinah shrieked. She fell back flat on the bed and twitched her legs in the air, like a dying grasshopper. "I don't *like* Nick, I *hate* him."

Suzanne gave a little shrug, as if to say, Think what you want if it makes you feel better. But I know the truth.

"Girls don't like boys who throw bras at them," Dinah said. She could make up laws of boy-girl behavior as well as Suzanne could.

"Sometimes they do, and sometimes they don't."

"That's right. Sometimes they *don't.*" It was past midnight. Dinah turned off the light and rolled over in bed.

"And sometimes they *do.*" Suzanne rolled over, too. And before Dinah could think of the perfect reply that would make Suzanne see how wrong she was about Nick, she could hear, from the regular, slow breathing in the bed next to hers, that Suzanne was asleep.

Dinah wore her new socks to school on Monday, a pink sock on her right foot, an orange sock on her left.

The socks attracted attention, all right. The girls asked her why her socks didn't match; the boys tried to think of various sock-related insults. Dinah answered them all with a publicity plug for the recycling sock hop on Friday, May 10.

Dinah wondered if Nick would say anything about her socks, or about their fight on Saturday. She didn't have to wait long. He was in homeroom before her, and as soon as she walked in, he bellowed across the room, "Nice socks, Ocean-River! But where's your hat? Last time I saw you, you were wearing some kind of pink lacy hat. It looked really great on you."

Dinah glared at Nick, a frigid stare that by all rights should have frozen him into a giant boy-shaped ice cube. Unfortunately, at the same time she felt herself blush.

"Dinah's blushing!" Nick announced loudly. The entire homeroom turned around to look.

"I am not!" Dinah said as every sixth grader whose last name began with the letters S through Z peered at her to see if what Nick had said was true.

"What size was that hat, anyway?" asked Nick. "A 38D?"

"Good morning," came a girl's voice over the public address system, saving Nick from a second attempt on his life. "Please rise and salute the flag." When the flag salute and morning announcements were over, Blaine Yarborough leaned over to Dinah and whispered, "What hat? What is Nick talking about?"

Dinah told her a four-minute version of the whole story on the way to their first-period class. When she

17

came to the end, she half expected Blaine to say, "He likes you," as Suzanne had; but instead Blaine said, "How gross. Katie Richards has a big crush on him, but I think Nick Tribble is disgusting."

"I think so, too," Dinah said.

Nick was in four of Dinah's classes—English, math, science, and social studies—as well as lunch. Dinah had never particularly noticed him in any of them before, but now it seemed she couldn't walk into a room without his being there, taller than the other boys, even taller than most of the girls, with a laugh that carried over the general classroom din and dark eyes that gleamed with mischief behind his sober, square-rimmed glasses.

In English class first period, Mr. Prensky sent students one by one to the chalkboard to diagram sentences. Usually he made them use sentences from the exercises in their *Fun with Grammar* workbook, but that day he let them diagram sentences of their own choosing, so long as each sentence had a dependent clause beginning with *who, which,* or *that.*

Dinah's sentence was: "I hate people who throw things at my head."

Nick's sentence was: "Pink hats look funny on girls that have frizzy hair."

In Dinah's view, if Mr. Prensky had been a normal human being, instead of a windup teaching mannequin, he would have shown some curiosity about these sentences.

Dinah, he could have said, what kind of things do

you have in mind, exactly? Has someone recently thrown something at your head?

To Nick he could have said: What exactly is so funny about a pink hat? And when did you develop such an interest in feminine headgear?

But all he said was, "*Who*, Mr. Tribble. On girls *who* have frizzy hair."

Actually, that wasn't the only error in Nick's sentence. Dinah's short, dark hair wasn't frizzy—it was curly. Which showed how much Nick Tribble knew about hats *or* hair.

Second-period gym was all girls, so Dinah should have been safe from any rude remarks for forty-seven minutes. Except that for the first time she realized that Nick had boys' gym the same period. The girls played softball on the diamond nearest the building; the boys played softball on the diamond laid out at the far end of the athletic field. But the field was a small one, and the two diamonds overlapped at their deepest point. So as fate would have it, when Dinah headed out to center field for the opening inning of the girls' softball game, there was Nick, glove in hand, taking center field for the boys.

"Here, Dinah, catch!" Nick tossed his glove at Dinah. "Try it on. Though I believe pink is your color."

The glove missed Dinah's head and fell harmlessly to the grass.

"Tribble!" The boys' gym teacher shouted across the field. "This is a ball game, not a tea party."

Dinah watched with satisfaction as Nick, scrambling

to retrieve his glove, missed the first ball hit to him. Later in the game, when Dinah struck out at bat, she heard a distant shout from the boys' field, "Way to go, Ocean-River!"

In science class, third period, Dinah hooked up dry-cell batteries, pretending to herself that she was using positive and negative electrodes to electrocute Nick. From what she could hear from Nick's lab table, two tables back, Nick was pretending to electrocute himself.

"Help! I'm frying! Now my hair will be frizzy like Dinah's!"

During math, Dinah managed to ignore Nick, but at lunch he sat at the table next to hers. Every time he caught her glancing at him, he opened his mouth wide to reveal its partially chewed contents.

"He is so *gross*," Blaine said.

"I know," Dinah said.

"He likes you," Suzanne said serenely.

"He does not!"

"A boy doesn't act gross like that around a girl unless he likes her."

Dinah looked at Blaine to see what she would make of Suzanne's pronouncement.

"If he does," Blaine said, "then I feel sorry for *you*, Dinah."

Blaine hadn't said that he *didn't*.

In social studies, sixth period, Mr. Dixon rapped on his desk with his pointer. He was a loud, blustery man, who shouted at his students as if they were his guests on a Sunday-morning TV talk show.

"Richards! No gum! Winfield! Let's keep our hands and feet to ourselves! Tribble! I think Richards is capable of removing her gum without any assistance from you."

"Richards" was Katie Richards, the girl who was supposed to like Nick, "too." What did it mean if Nick was trying to remove her chewing gum? Dinah didn't turn around to find out. She really couldn't care less whether Nick liked Katie or not.

"Class!" Mr. Dixon bellowed. "Today I'm going to assign your major project for this marking period." He picked up the chalk and wrote a single word, DEBATES, on the board with such emphasis that the chalk snapped in half in his hand. But Mr. Dixon's class was used to breaking chalk and flying erasers.

"Each of you will be debating an issue of the day, here in front of your classmates, with a partner. One of you will argue the affirmative, the other the negative. I will assign partners, topics, and dates. Assignments are final. Get it?"

The class was silent.

"You got it. All right, kiddoes, here goes. May seventh. Resolved: The sale of handguns should be strictly controlled. Affirmative, Artie Adams. Negative, Blaine Yarborough."

Poor Artie. Dinah knew from the class elections last fall that Blaine was a wonderful debater—logical, clear, organized, and forceful. Blaine was the presidential type through and through, as Dinah had learned the hard way when she ran against her for class president.

"May eighth. Resolved: The use of marijuana, heroin,

and cocaine should be legalized. Affirmative, Katie Richards. Negative, Jason Winfield.

"May nineth. Resolved: Capital punishment should be abolished. Affirmative, Nick Tribble. Negative, Dinah Seabrooke.

"May tenth—"

Katie Richards was waving her hand in the air.

"Richards?"

"But what if— I mean, I *don't* think drugs should be legal. I think people should just say no to drugs."

"You will be spending the next month studying the art of debating," Mr. Dixon said, "as well as researching your own particular topic. A good debater doesn't have to believe personally in the position he or she defends. He or she just has to be able to make the strongest possible case for it."

"My parents aren't going to want me saying that drugs are good," Katie persisted. She sounded close to tears.

"I'm not asking you to argue that drugs are good," Mr. Dixon said, "but that drugs do less damage if their use is legal." He sighed. "Winfield? Would you be willing to switch sides with Richards?"

"Sure," Jason said.

"Thank you. The rest of you, try to do your best with the topic as given. May tenth . . . "

Dinah didn't mind her topic; it was her partner she wanted to change. But she couldn't very well raise her hand and say her parents wouldn't let her debate someone as gross as Nick Tribble. As for the topic,

Dinah's parents both believed in capital punishment, and Dinah did, too—especially in the case of someone who threw a bra at someone else's head, or made fun of her curly hair, or called her Ocean-River when her name was Seabrooke.

3

After school that day Dinah and Suzanne stayed for a special meeting of the Drama Club, for sixth graders only. Back in September Dinah had been thrilled at the thought of joining a club that put on real plays, but Drama Club had turned out to be one of middle school's biggest disappointments. First there had been the fall play, *You're a Good Man, Charlie Brown,* a musical based on the comic strip *Peanuts.* Any impartial observer would have had to admit that Dinah was born to play Lucy. She looked like Lucy, she acted like Lucy, she might have been Lucy's twin sister. But was Dinah picked to be Lucy? No. An eighth-grade girl with straight *blond* hair was picked to be Lucy instead. Mrs. Bevens, the drama coach, said it was because Stephanie could sing, and "Dinah, dear, I think you may be just the tiniest bit tone-deaf." So Stephanie got the starring role, while Dinah toiled backstage as a member of the stage crew.

"Well, it *is* a musical," Dinah's own father had said, siding with Mrs. Bevens. "I suppose singing is important."

Hadn't they ever heard of lip-syncing? Stephanie could have stood in the wings singing Lucy's songs while Dinah paraded up and down the stage, moving her mouth in time to the music. It was done all the time in rock videos.

Then there had been the disappointment about morning announcements. This semester Drama Club members were leading the Pledge of Allegiance and reading the school's announcements over the public address system every morning, a different student each week. Leading the Pledge of Allegiance wasn't the same thing as starring in a play, but Dinah had looked forward to her week nonetheless. With twenty whole weeks in the semester, why had that been the week she came down with the flu? Dinah's turn at morning announcements had been postponed until early May, still a whole month away.

Dinah's last hope for the Drama Club rested on the spring one-act plays. The sixth grade, seventh grade, and eighth grade were each to perform a short play in an assembly for the rest of the students in their grades. It would be a lot easier to get a good part now that Dinah didn't have to compete against the big kids. What if she didn't get one? But she would. It wasn't bragging to say that she had real talent as an actress, because she did. According to Dinah's father, some famous baseball player used to say, "Braggin's only when you ain't got nothin' to back it up."

Dinah and Suzanne sat together toward the front of the room with the other sixth graders, mostly girls. For some reason, more girls than boys joined Drama Club.

Jason and Artie weren't members, or Nick—thank goodness for that. So far only two sixth-grade boys had come for the one-act-play auditions: a short, stocky boy named Paul Hatfield, and Todd Burstyn, a serious boy who was in several of Dinah's classes. Todd and Paul were practically guaranteed the two best boys' parts. It wasn't fair.

"We could play boys' parts, too, you know," Dinah whispered to Suzanne. "If I wore my false nose, with the mustache and glasses, I'd look as much like a boy as Todd and Paul. And you could put your hair up under a cap."

"But I heard the sixth-grade play is going to be a romance," Suzanne said. "It even has a kiss in it."

A kiss?

"There's a boy who's the villain, and a boy who's the hero, and the hero and the main girl kiss at the end."

"I'm not kissing Paul or Todd," Dinah said. "I mean, would you?"

"If it was just in a play, I would. I'd pretend that it was Greg." Suzanne grinned slyly. "And you could pretend it was Nick."

"I'd rather kiss a snake," Dinah sputtered. "Or a scorpion. Or a viper. Or a cold, clammy, slimy, bug-eyed frog."

"Frogs turn out to be princes sometimes," Suzanne pointed out.

But Dinah didn't want to kiss a prince, either. Dinah wasn't the type to kiss frogs *or* princes, particularly if the princes were sixth-grade boys.

As a couple of latecomers straggled in, Mrs. Bevens passed out copies of the play, *Love Saves the Day; or, Virtue Triumphs over Villainy*. Quickly Dinah scanned the cast list. The play had six parts, three for boys and three for girls.

"*Love Saves the Day* is called a *melodrama*," Mrs. Bevens explained, writing the word on the chalkboard. "It has exaggerated characters and situations that are meant to be comical, as well as dramatic and exciting. These are parts you can really ham up. We want to have our audience cheering the hero and heroine and hissing and booing the villain—all in fun, of course. I think you should have a good time with this one."

Mrs. Bevens copied the cast list onto the board. "I was hoping more boys would try out," she said. Though Dinah counted nine girls, Paul and Todd were still the only boys in the room. "Do any of you have any male friends who might be interested? We really need at least one more."

"A girl could play one of the boys' parts," Dinah called out, forgetting to raise her hand. "The way a girl played Snoopy in *You're a Good Man, Charlie Brown*." That was another sore point with Dinah: She hadn't been cast as Snoopy, either.

"I suppose so," Mrs. Bevens said. "After all, in Shakespeare's time all parts, male and female, were played by men—Desdemona, Ophelia, Juliet. But maybe we can rustle up some more boys by this time next week."

Mrs. Bevens was probably old enough to have lived in Shakespeare's time and gone to the opening nights of all his plays. It was no wonder that she didn't know about lip-syncing in rock videos.

"All right, let's start the auditions," Mrs. Bevens went on. "Suzanne, why don't you read for Olivia, our heroine, and Todd, let's hear you as Manly, our handsome hero."

Suzanne and Todd took their places in the front of the room and began to read aloud from the scene Mrs. Bevens had selected. Suzanne read well, her voice sweet and clear; Todd spoke too softly, but managed to get through Manly's lines without stumbling. Dinah hardly listened. As Suzanne and Todd read on, Dinah imagined herself executing deeds of great daring and wickedness, while in the darkened auditorium two hundred sixth graders hissed and booed and stomped their feet. She would forgive Mrs. Bevens for letting others play Lucy and Snoopy if only she could be Wilfredo Desperado, the black-mustachioed villain of *Love Saves the Day*.

On the way home from the auditions, Dinah got off the bus a few stops early to visit her friend Mrs. Briscoe. Mrs. Briscoe had started out as a client of Dinah's mother, who was an organization consultant, but had ended up as Dinah's friend. It might seem odd to some people that Dinah's second-best friend, after Suzanne, was an eighty-three-year-old lady, but Dinah loved having a friend who was a grown-up but not a parent—somebody who was wise and understanding, but who didn't get upset by the little things that tended to upset mothers and fathers.

When she had been younger, Dinah had told her parents every detail about all of her adventures, but now that she was in middle school she found herself leaving out parts of stories. For instance, she hadn't told her parents that Nick Tribble had thrown a *bra* at her head. She had a feeling they wouldn't like a story that had both a boy *and* a bra in it.

But when she told the full story to Mrs. Briscoe that afternoon, all Mrs. Briscoe said was "Oh, my."

"Did anybody ever throw—well, something like that at you?" Dinah asked.

"No, I can't say that anyone did. Of course, in my day we were all much more straitlaced about such things. But now that you mention it, one young man did throw a corsage at me once, and his aim wasn't very good, or else I wasn't very good at catching, and it struck me in the face and knocked my glasses off— knocked them clear across the room—broke the frames and smashed one of the lenses."

"What happened then? Were you mad? Did you ever see him again?"

"I married him. That was my Eddie. Mr. Briscoe."

"Oh," Dinah said. It sounded a little lame, so she changed it to "Oh, my."

She told Mrs. Briscoe about the debate. Mrs. Briscoe was in favor of capital punishment, too.

"At least I suppose I am," Mrs. Briscoe said. "Though

I have to say, sometimes my heart goes out to those poor wretches waiting for years and years on death row, hoping for a miracle right up to the day of the execution."

"Well, they should have thought of that before they killed somebody," Dinah said. "The person they killed probably hoped for a miracle, too, and it didn't happen."

"Spoken like a true debater!" Mrs. Briscoe said approvingly.

Dinah told Mrs. Briscoe about the play, and Mrs. Briscoe agreed that Dinah would be perfect as Wilfredo Desperado.

"This Nick Tribble, is he going to be in the play, too?" Mrs. Briscoe asked. "He sounds like a bit of the Wilfredo Desperado type himself."

"No," Dinah said. "At least, I hope not." Out of Mrs. Briscoe's front window she saw her father's car. "My dad's here. I have to go."

"Watch out for flying objects!" Mrs. Briscoe called after her. But a flying corsage and a flying bra were entirely different.

Once home, Dinah pounced on her baby brother, Benjamin, and gave him a big tickling hug. In his denim overalls and red-checked shirt, Benjamin looked like a small, chubby farmhand on Old Mac-Donald's farm.

"I-I!" he shouted. It was his way of saying *Dinah*. Benjamin was Dinah's favorite person in the whole world, proving that there was at least one boy she liked.

At dinner Dinah told her parents about the play. Then she said, "Remember that boy who was bothering me in the store on Saturday? Well, he bothered me at school all day today, too. And Mr. Dixon assigned him to be my opponent in our big classroom debate on capital punishment. He's supposed to be against it, and I'm supposed to be in favor of it."

Dinah's mother frowned. "Do your best to avoid him," she advised Dinah. "These past few months have been so trouble-free—I don't think the school has had to phone us once. It would be a shame if— Well, it's nice to think we're making some progress."

But her father grinned. "I spent five years bothering you, Judy, and you bothered me right back, and we both had a fine time of it."

Benjamin grabbed hold of his spoon, stuck it into his bowl of baby-food squash, and aimed it at his right eye. Dinah's mother leaned over and helped guide the spoon into his mouth, or near enough to his mouth that the excess squash fell onto his bib rather than onto his tangle of yellow curls.

"Don't encourage her, Jerry," she said. "A little encouragement goes a long way with Dinah. Tell us more about the play, honey. Are parents invited? Will we be able to come?"

"Probably," Dinah said. "But remember, I don't have the part yet."

"You'll get something wonderful this time," her mother predicted. "If you can just manage to stay out of trouble. Oh, Benjamin!"

Benjamin had emptied his bowl onto his head. Great rivulets of bright orange squash ran down his forehead onto his cheeks and nose. Dinah's mother rescued the bowl before it tumbled onto the plastic mat under the high chair, and her father ran for the sponge.

"May I be excused?" Dinah asked. She slipped away from the table without waiting for an answer. At times it was highly convenient having a baby brother.

4

"Calling all sixth-grade boys!" came the announcement over the PA system Tuesday morning. To think
that, in another month, the voice booming over the
speakers would be none other than Dinah's own.

"Auditions for the sixth-grade class play, *Love Saves
the Day*, will be held again this Thursday after school
in room one twenty-seven. Come try out for the roles
of handsome, daring hero Manly Allweather, lost heir
Humphrey Montpelier, and evil villain Wilfredo
Desperado!"

Dinah peered around her homeroom to see if any of
the boys were listening. In front of her, Jason Winfield
was inking in an elaborate sports scene on the cover of
his social studies book. The boy who sat behind her
had his head down on his desk, pretending to be
asleep.

Dinah looked at Nick and caught him looking at her.

"What part are you going to be?" he mouthed across
the room at her.

How did he know she was in the Drama Club?

Dinah looked away, but when the bell rang, Nick caught up with her in the hallway.

"You *are* trying out for the play, aren't you?" he asked. "Artie said you were always in plays last year."

"What's it to you?" Dinah asked coldly.

"I have to get some ripe tomatoes ready if you are, that's all. Or maybe rotten eggs. No, honestly, I might try out for the play myself."

"Don't bother," Dinah told him. "There are two boys trying out already, and they can be Manly and Humphrey. Mrs. Bevens is going to give the part of Wilfredo Desperado to a girl. She practically said so yesterday. Girls acted boys' parts all the time in Shakespeare's plays, you know." Well, vice versa, but the principle was the same.

"Which girl?" Nick asked. "Which girl is going to play Wilfredo?"

"Never mind."

"Her name wouldn't happen to be Dynamite Ocean-River, would it?"

"No," Dinah said. Seabrooke, yes. Ocean-River, definitely not.

"It's funny that they made that announcement, though, isn't it?" Nick asked. "Calling all *boys*. I don't know, Ocean-River. I wouldn't count your chickens before they're hatched. One of those eggs might turn out to have a stinkorific surprise in it. Thursday, she said? Room one twenty-seven? See you later, Atlantic-Mississippi."

Nick grinned at Dinah as they took their seats in

first-period English. Dinah returned his grin with a glare. Nick wouldn't *dare* try out for Dinah's chosen role in the play. And if he did, well, Dinah would just have to prove to Mrs. Bevens that the part was rightfully hers, even if she wasn't a boy.

"You'll be Olivia," Dinah told Suzanne after school Wednesday afternoon, as they sat in Suzanne's kitchen eating M&M's together.

Suzanne shook her head. "*You'll* be Olivia."

"But I don't want to be. I want to be Wilfredo."

"They'll find a boy for Wilfredo, and you'll be Olivia, because it's the best girl's part, and you should have been Lucy except that you can't sing. I'll be the mother. I'm the mother type."

Dinah wet her finger and touched it to an orange M&M. Then she carefully stuck the M&M in the middle of her forehead.

"You're the Olivia type, too," Dinah said. "You read the best of anybody for Olivia last time."

"*You* read the best," Suzanne said.

Dinah tried to look modest. Actually, she thought she had read remarkably well for Olivia, and if a boy did get the part of Wilfredo, well, Olivia was by far the grandest girl's part. There was no doubt about that. On the other hand, Suzanne *was* the Olivia type. Suzanne was sweet and kind and unselfish, just like the heroine of *Love Saves the Day*. Dinah wasn't selfish, exactly, but she wasn't *un*selfish, either.

"Of course," Suzanne said, "Mrs. Bevens might not

give Olivia to either of us. She might give it to Mandy Bricker or Heather Allen."

"She better not," Dinah said. "If I don't get it, I want you to get it."

"If I don't get it, I want *you* to get it," Suzanne said.

"You'll be Olivia, and I'll be Wilfredo," Dinah insisted. "Unless—"

The orange M&M fell off Dinah's forehead, onto the Kellys' oak kitchen table.

"I don't think Nick is really going to try out," Suzanne said. "He was just teasing you. You know how boys tease girls when they like them."

Dinah refused to dignify that with an answer. She only hoped that this time Suzanne was right.

But when Dinah and Suzanne hurried to the audition the next afternoon, Nick was there before them, sitting in the first desk in the first row, intently studying the script for *Love Saves the Day.*

"Marry me, my pretty one, and your mortgage is forgotten," he greeted Dinah in a deep, villainous voice.

"I will not marry one I do not love," Dinah replied without missing a beat, remembering the line from Monday's tryouts.

"Then I will find another way to make you mine," Nick read on. "I will not rest until you change your name from Ocean-River to Desperado."

"Then you will never rest this side of the grave," Dinah shot back. She had a good memory for lines. Once, in fifth grade, she had memorized a poem that was two hundred lines long. She used to recite it for Benjamin when he was fussing in his walker.

Dinah was suddenly aware that, from the doorway, Mrs. Bevens was watching them. As usual, her face revealed no expression. Was Mrs. Bevens thinking that Nick would make a good Wilfredo? Or that Dinah would make a good Olivia? Or both?

It might be fun to play Olivia, after all, with Nick as Wilfredo. But then Suzanne would lose any chance at a starring role. It would definitely be better if Suzanne played Olivia and Dinah played Wilfredo. Maybe Nick could play Manly, the handsome hero. But there was something about the thought of Nick kissing Suzanne that made Dinah feel—not odd, really; but it was just hard to imagine the two of them together.

Todd Burstyn and Paul Hatfield arrived a few minutes later, joined this time by two boys Dinah didn't know— two more competitors for Wilfredo. Last time Dinah had counted nine girls; this time there were eleven. Competition would be keen for any of the girls' parts: Olivia, her aging mother, and the Gypsy fortune-teller.

Though a small role, the fortune-teller had some good lines. If worse came to worst, and Nick played Wilfredo with Suzanne as Olivia, Dinah might be able to shine as the half-crazy crone who stalked the stage muttering, "Mark well these words. What is, is not. And what is not will come to be." Even the mother's role would be better than nothing. Dinah could study Mrs. Briscoe's inflections and mannerisms as a guide for bringing Olivia's dignified elderly mother to life.

Dinah never felt more tense than when other people were trying out for parts she wanted. As each of the other girls stood up to read, she dug her chewed-off fingernails into the palms of her tightly clenched fists. Several of the girls read badly, delivering their lines in a flat singsong, or with phony, exaggerated feeling. But several read quite well, including Suzanne. Dinah loved Suzanne, and she wanted Suzanne to be a star—but not quite as starry a star as Dinah herself.

Nick read well for Wilfredo, but he was the only boy who did. Neither he nor Todd nor Paul had anything to fear from the newcomers, whose names were sure to appear at the bottom of the cast list as backstage crew. Nick read well as Manly, too, and so did Todd. Paul, chubby and cherub faced, was perfect for the role of young Humphrey Montpelier, Olivia's ward and the long-lost heir of the vast Montpelier fortune.

As the audition dragged on, Dinah waved her hand.

"Don't forget, you said a girl could play Wilfredo," she said.

"Don't worry, dear," Mrs. Bevens said. "You read for Wilfredo last time, and I remember your scene perfectly. But now I'd like to hear you as Olivia with—" Mrs. Bevens glanced around the room. "Nick, let's hear you again for Manly."

This was a possibility Dinah had overlooked.

If Dinah played Olivia and Nick played Manly, what would they do about the closing scene—the one with the kiss?

"All right, you two," Mrs. Bevens said. "Start reading at the top of page fifty-nine."

Dinah turned in her script to the page Mrs. Bevens wanted and glanced down at Olivia's lines. It helped to skim a scene first before speaking the lines aloud.

Then Dinah stopped, stunned with a horrifying realization. The play ended on page sixty. *This* was the closing scene. There, on the bottom of the page, she read the unmistakable stage directions: "Manly takes Olivia in his arms and kisses her."

No. Mrs. Bevens didn't expect them to kiss in a try-out. They were supposed to read the lines, not act them out. Certainly they weren't supposed to *kiss* each other, a real kiss full on the lips. Dinah knew that.

Did Nick?

"Nick, Dinah, let's get started," Mrs. Bevens said.

Slowly Dinah left her seat and walked to the front of the classroom. She couldn't make herself look at Nick. But maybe he hadn't read ahead in his script. Maybe he didn't know what lay in store for them both.

Olivia had the first line. "Oh, Manly," Dinah read.

"Yes, my dear?" Nick as Manly replied.

(Olivia raises her downcast eyes and looks at Manly for the first time.)

Dinah raised her downcast eyes and looked at Nick. He knew what was coming, all right. No one who wasn't plotting mischief could look that innocent.

"You—you saved my farm. You saved my honor. You saved . . . my life. How can I ever thank you?"

"I did not do it for your thanks."

"Then, why? You risked all for me. I must give you something in return."

"I ask only . . . your love."

Nick's voice was shaking. With nervousness, or with suppressed laughter? Dinah didn't know if she could go on reading. She felt like dropping her script and fleeing the room. But she was too good an actress to retreat. A true actress wouldn't be stopped even by the prospect of a kiss from Nick Tribble.

Dinah lifted her chin and read on. "If you want so poor a thing, it is yours!"

(Manly takes Olivia in his arms and kisses her.)

Nick took Dinah in his arms. At least, he grabbed hold of her and awkwardly tilted her back. Back, back, so far that every bone in Dinah's spine felt the strain. Nick's face was bent to hers, close enough that she could see his glasses slipping down his nose and felt his warm breath on her neck.

Dinah closed her eyes to block out what was coming next.

Unfortunately, she didn't cover her ears. Nick burped. It was a gigantic burp, a burp to end all burps, a burp to wake the dead, a burp heard round the world.

Dinah tried to get free of Nick's hold, but he was laughing so hard that they both lost their balance and fell into a tangled heap on the dusty classroom floor.

"Nicholas!" Mrs. Bevens called out, majestic in her fury.

Nick scrambled up. "Gee, I'm sorry. Really, I am. I guess I drank too much Coke or something. I mean, it just kind of *happened*."

"Nicholas!"

"Okay, I know I should have said, 'Excuse me,' but— You don't think I did it on *purpose?*"

Dinah lay on the floor, her eyes still closed. Maybe her back was broken. Maybe she would be paralyzed for life, and it would all be Nick Tribble's fault, and he would get the electric chair. Causing lifelong paralysis was practically as bad as murder. Dinah wiggled her toes tentatively. They still moved. But even if her toes weren't paralyzed, the rest of her might be.

"Hey, Ocean-River, are you okay?" Nick's voice sounded different. The laughter had gone out of it.

Dinah opened one eye. Nick was leaning over her. He looked genuinely worried.

"I think my back is broken," Dinah whispered faintly. She closed her eyes again.

"Dinah, wake up. Listen to me. Okay, I meant to burp, but I didn't mean to drop you. Honest, I didn't."

Dinah moaned.

Then she heard Mrs. Bevens's voice directly above her, impatient, no-nonsense. "Get up, Dinah." This time Mrs. Bevens forgot to add the "dear."

How did Mrs. Bevens know Dinah's back wasn't really broken? Dinah herself didn't know that yet. She eased herself carefully into a sitting position. Okay, Mrs. Bevens was right. Dinah's back *wasn't* broken. What a disappointment.

"Here." Nick held out his hand.

Dinah ignored it. Unaided, she rose to her feet.

"Audition dismissed," Mrs. Bevens said. "I'll post the cast list after eighth period on Monday."

As Dinah left the room with Suzanne, she heard Nick still in conference with Mrs. Bevens.

"I mean, don't *you* burp sometimes? Even teachers burp *sometimes*."

5

"Mr. Briscoe never burped in your face when he was supposed to kiss you, did he?" Dinah asked Mrs. Briscoe later that afternoon. She had promised she'd stop by for a quick report after the audition.

"No," Mrs. Briscoe said. "Definitely not. My memory may be fading, but on that point I'm absolutely certain."

Dinah swallowed a sip of lemony tea and took a bite of buttered toast.

"But wait," Mrs. Briscoe said. "There *was* some mix-up involving a kiss. That's right. It's coming back to me. I still haven't forgiven Eddie for it completely, and he's been gone ten years now."

"What happened?" Dinah had to know.

"It was at a cornhusking. Eddie and I grew up in a small farming community, and in those days we'd all get together in the fall to husk our corn. We'd make a party of it. We never lacked an excuse for a party back then. Well, you know about husking bees, don't you? You know what happens when a fellow gets a red ear of corn?"

Dinah shook her head.

"He can kiss any girl he likes. And I mean to tell you, half those young men spent more time looking for a red ear than they did husking the rest."

"So Mr. Briscoe found a red ear and he kissed you?"

"You're half right. He found a red ear, or, rather, it found him. I'm sure Eddie wasn't looking for it. But as soon as those red kernels appeared, a great cry went up all around him. He looked right across the room at me, and I blushed redder than that corn. So Eddie stood up, and everyone was hooting and hollering, and he started across the room toward me, the red ear still in his hand. And my heart was pounding away, because I'd never been kissed before, I don't mind admitting it. We waited longer to start with the kissing in my day.

"Closer he came, closer—looking right at me—and then I closed my eyes, but kept my face turned up, so he could reach my mouth without a lot of fuss and fumbling. I must have been a foolish sight."

"And then he kissed you?"

"No. Then he *didn't* kiss me."

"He kissed someone else?"

"No, he handed that red ear to Owen Kellogg, sitting right next to me, and Owen lost no time kissing *his* girl. I'm surprised I'm not still sitting there, my face puckered up, waiting."

"Why didn't he kiss you? I mean, he married you, right?"

"Shyness, I expect. And maybe just the slightest bit of mischief, too. Why didn't your Nick Tribble kiss you?"

"Grossness," Dinah said. "Pure, hideous grossness."

Mrs. Briscoe patted Dinah's hand. "Shyness can take different forms, you know."

Dinah shook her head. "There's no such thing," she said, "as a shy burp."

Dinah hadn't meant to tell her parents about Nick's burp, but they asked about the audition at dinner, and the story was only half a story without it.

"Is this that same boy who's been bothering you?" her mother asked.

"Uh-huh. The one who's my partner in the social studies debate."

"Jerry, do you think we ought to speak to Dinah's teacher? And see if he can change the assignment so she's paired with someone else?"

Dinah had a sudden twinge of panic. The last thing she wanted was her parents calling her teachers. Besides, she almost wanted to debate Nick. It would be easy to argue in favor of capital punishment, given how strongly she already felt about it. Forced to argue the weaker side, Nick would be thoroughly trounced. Dinah wanted to be the one to do the trouncing.

Dinah's father wiped a streak of pureed peas from Benjamin's forehead. "I think Dinah's going to live. Am I right, Dinah? But what I still want to know is, who are you going to invite to your sock dance?"

"Benjamin," Dinah replied automatically. Actually, she wasn't as opposed to inviting a boy as she had been a week ago, so long as the boy wasn't Nick. Since everyone seemed to expect her to invite Nick, it would be satisfying to announce that she had invited someone else.

"Speaking of Benjamin," Dinah's mother said. She cleared her throat and looked significantly at Dinah's father.

"Ah-ha," he said. "Dinah, your mother and I have tickets for a concert this weekend. Would you like to baby-sit for Benjamin on Saturday afternoon?"

"All by myself?"

"Unless Suzanne wants to sit with you. Otherwise, yes, by yourself. We'd pay you two dollars an hour."

"Suzanne has a piano recital on Saturday. But you know I'd like to baby-sit for Benjamin. I'd like it more than anything."

Dinah was overjoyed. For months she had been begging her parents to let her baby-sit, but they always said she wasn't "mature" enough. Which meant that when her parents went out, Dinah herself had to have a baby-sitter, even though she was practically twelve, and half the girls her age were already baby-sitting for money. Dinah thought there were few occupations more glamorous than that of baby-sitter. Of course, sitting for your own brother wasn't as exciting as sitting for a stranger. But two dollars an hour was two dollars an hour, whoever paid you.

"Now, Dinah, this is an experiment," her mother said. "We think you're ready for this responsibility, but it's up to you to prove us right."

Dinah swooped down on Benjamin for a sticky kiss,

almost knocking his bowl of peas to the floor in the process.

"We're ready, aren't we, Benjamin?"

Her career as a world-famous living mannequin hadn't worked out, thanks to Nick. It was high time she launched a new career as a world-famous baby-sitter.

Since Dinah's mother was an organization consultant, she was a specialist in organizing things. So the instructions she left Dinah on Saturday afternoon were a model of clearness and completeness.

Dinah's parents reviewed the list with her one last time before they dressed for the concert. Then they posted it on the refrigerator door.

BABY-SITTING IS A SERIOUS BUSINESS!
1. You may answer the phone. But don't talk more than three minutes.
2. Don't open the door to strangers.
3. Don't let anyone inside the house.
4. Take Benjamin for a walk if you like, but be sure to lock the door when you go.
5. And take your key with you!

The list went on and on—instructions about Benjamin's bottle, about his cereal, about his diapers, about the need to keep him from tumbling down the stairs.

"You didn't put 'Don't play with matches,'" Dinah told her mother as she accepted her good-bye kiss.

"Does that mean we can play with matches if we want?"

"Dinah!"

"Just joking," Dinah put in quickly.

"Don't joke!" her parents said together.

Her mother still looked worried, so Dinah struck a dramatic pose. "Have no fear, Dinah is here!"

"Jerry, are you sure we should go? Dinah's too young. She's too— She has too many *ideas*."

With a wink to Dinah, her father steered her mother out the door. Dinah heard the car engine turn over. From the window she and Benjamin watched their parents' car back slowly out the driveway.

Dinah's first job as a world-famous baby-sitter had begun.

For a while Dinah and Benjamin played with Benjamin's plastic snap-together blocks. Dinah would build a tower for Benjamin; he would jam it into his mouth and slobber on it. Then Dinah did "This little piggy" with Benjamin's short, stubby toes. She played peekaboo. She read *Pat the Bunny*. She sang all the verses of "Old MacDonald Had a Farm."

She looked at the clock on the kitchen microwave. Her parents had left at 3:00. It was now 3:20.

Dinah sang all the verses of "This Old Man, He Played One."

3:25.

Maybe it was time for Benjamin's nap. But he had already had his nap. And it was too early for bottle and cereal.

Baby-sitting, it was turning out, was almost as boring

as being a living mannequin. Maybe all jobs were boring once you had done them for more than ten minutes. Maybe the president of the United States spent a lot of time staring at his watch, waiting for something interesting to happen.

The doorbell rang. *Don't open the door to strangers.* Certainly not. But how would Dinah know if it *was* a stranger without checking? She stuck Benjamin into his high chair and ran for the kitchen step stool. By standing on it, she'd be able to look out the glass pane at the top of the door to see who was on the other side.

But when she peered out, she saw nobody. When she asked, "Who is it?" no one answered.

"I-I!" Benjamin shouted from the kitchen.

"I'm coming!" Dinah called.

Just then the doorbell rang again. The stool was still in place. Dinah peeked out. Again, nobody. But this time she had looked out so quickly that she knew the person ringing hadn't had time to give up and walk away. He had *run* away. On purpose. To play a joke on whoever answered the door. But where had he run to that Dinah couldn't see him? He must be hiding in the bushes at the front of the house.

It was a bit scary to think of someone hiding in her bushes. But Dinah had a feeling the prankster wasn't a dangerous criminal. She had a feeling it was someone from school, someone she knew.

From outside the door, Dinah heard a boy's voice, singing. She opened the living room window to hear better.

"I dream of Dinah with the frizzy hair!" the boy

49

sang, to the tune of "Jeanie with the Light Brown Hair," which they sang in eighth-period music class at school.

Dinah raised the screen and poked her head out. Sure enough, something moved in the bushes next to the front door. Dinah knew her visitor had to be Nick. If only the little squirter hose from the kitchen sink could reach all the way out the living room window. But there was a long outdoor hose in the backyard.

"I-I! I-I!" Benjamin continued to chant.

"Just a minute!"

Dinah raced through the kitchen and out the kitchen door, pulling the door carefully shut behind her so that if Benjamin somehow wriggled out of his high chair, he couldn't escape. She was proud to have thought of her baby-sitting responsibilities even when there was a bush so urgently in need of watering.

At the back of the house, Dinah turned the hose on at the faucet, but turned off the nozzle. Then, dragging the hose behind her, she crept around to the front yard.

"Dinah, Dinah, give me your answer true!" the bush was singing now. "Your hair is frizzy! Your feet are gigantic, too!"

Dinah took aim at the center of the bush and twisted the nozzle of the hose. A powerful jet of icy-cold water shot out.

Yelling, Nick ran from behind the bush and tried to wrestle the hose away from Dinah. In a minute, Dinah was completely drenched, soaked to the skin. The April breeze blew briskly, and she felt half frozen. But it had been worth it to hear Nick's first yelp of painful surprise.

Finally, Dinah managed to get the hose turned off.

"You can go now," she told Nick through chattering teeth.

"Aren't you going to invite me in?" Nick asked. "I might freeze to death out here."

"Are you kidding? I wouldn't if I could. Besides, I can't. I'm baby-sitting. I'm not supposed to let anyone in. My parents said so." It was on the rule list: *Don't let anyone inside the house.*

Suddenly Dinah remembered another rule on the list. If she went outside, she was supposed to lock the door and take the key with her. Dinah hadn't taken her key. And she had pulled the kitchen door shut so firmly. And when the kitchen door shut, it locked.

Dinah could hear Benjamin. He was crying now, hard.

"I think—I think I'm locked out," Dinah said in a small, strangled voice.

Nick didn't laugh. "Let's try the door."

He followed Dinah to the back of the house. Sure enough, the kitchen door wouldn't budge.

"Do your parents have an extra key hidden outside somewhere?" Nick asked. "My parents keep one under a fake rock next to the front walk."

Dinah shook her head.

"Do any neighbors have a key?"

"The Harmons. Next door."

Dinah ran across the yard and pounded at the Harmons' back door. But she knew it was no use. Their station wagon wasn't in the driveway. They were obviously away for the afternoon.

"The front window!" Dinah said. "I left it open." She had opened it far enough to stick her head out to spy on Nick. Would that be far enough for one of them to climb through?

"We can get in," Nick said when he saw it. "Do you want me to try it, or should I give you a boost?"

"You can do it." Dinah had many talents, but performing acrobatics wasn't one of them. She wasn't supposed to let anyone in the house, but then again, she wasn't supposed to have locked herself out of the house in the first place. The important thing now was just to get inside and comfort Benjamin.

The window was higher than Nick's shoulder, but he found a foothold in the bush next to it and hoisted himself to the sill. Nimbly, he eased himself feetfirst through the opening. A moment later, he had the front door open, and Dinah flew to the kitchen to rescue Benjamin, still howling, from his high chair.

"I guess I'd better go," Nick said then.

"Your clothes are still wet."

"I'll be okay. I don't live very far—just over on Barclay Court. It was a good thing you left that window open."

Dinah nodded, looking at the window. Then she noticed an alarmingly large puddle of water on the hardwood floor, left over from the hose fight.

"See you Monday, Ocean-River," Nick said. "Fifty cents says I get Wilfredo Desperado and you don't."

Then he was gone. And good riddance, too. Nick had been nice for a few minutes—surprisingly nice—but Dinah was mad at him, anyway. Another promising career ruined. Not that Dinah could say that the afternoon had provided stellar evidence of her maturity and responsibleness. More the opposite, really.

Dinah changed into dry clothes and hung her wet ones on the shower rod in the bathroom. Then, with Benjamin balanced awkwardly on her hip, she went downstairs to the basement to get the mop.

6

"Oh, Dinah," her mother said that evening when Dinah made herself confess the baby-sitting disaster.

"You don't have to pay me," Dinah offered. "At least not for the time I was outside having the hose fight with Nick. You can subtract for that part."

"I think we'd better subtract for the whole thing," her father said. "It looks like we'll be paying teenage baby-sitters for a long while yet."

"This Nick, the one you had the hose fight with," Dinah's mother said. "Is he the same one who—"

"Yes," Dinah said.

Her mother just sighed again, but Dinah thought her father hid a smile as he bent to check the living room floor for water damage.

On Sunday afternoon Dinah and Suzanne went to the public library together. Suzanne's social studies teacher had assigned reports on foreign countries; Suzanne was doing hers on Poland. Dinah wanted to start working on the capital punishment debate for Mr. Dixon. It was the first really warm day of the spring.

Overnight all the daffodils had bloomed, standing tall and slender amid carpets of purple crocuses grown wild as weeds.

By the time they reached the library, Suzanne had heard the whole baby-sitting story, and the girls had reviewed every possible choice for the cast of *Love Saves the Day*.

"Nick will be Wilfredo, you'll be Olivia, and I'll be the mother," Suzanne concluded.

"Nick will be Wilfredo, *you'll* be Olivia, and I'll be the Gypsy fortune-teller," Dinah concluded. But she hoped she was wrong. She still pictured the cast list in her mind:

Wilfredo Desperado . . . . . . Dinah Seabrooke

Either way, she would know by 3:18 on Monday.

The library was crowded with old people reading the Sunday newspapers and students busy with schoolwork due on Monday. Dinah's debate was still a few weeks away, but she wanted to give herself plenty of time to prepare.

Basically, though, she already knew what she was going to say. There had to be capital punishment, or else murderers might get out of prison on parole and kill again. And if you knew you'd get the death penalty for killing someone else, you'd definitely think twice before you did it. Besides, somebody who killed somebody else deserved to be killed. It wouldn't be fair for a murderer to go on living when the murdered person was dead.

Dinah sat down in front of the long shelf of *The Reader's Guide to Periodical Literature*. They had just learned how to use *The Reader's Guide* last week in the school library. Now Dinah opened the fat volume for the past year and turned to the entry on capital punishment. Sure enough, there were several articles listed, from different magazines. She opened her notebook and started copying the list. This was going to be easy. Already Dinah sniffed victory in the air.

But an hour later Dinah was discouraged. It was one thing to find an article listed in *The Reader's Guide*. It was another thing to find the article itself. Half the time it turned out that the Riverdale Library didn't subscribe to the periodical she was looking for. Or the issue Dinah wanted was missing. Or the issue was there, but the article mysteriously failed to appear. Or the article, when Dinah finally pounced on it, was only a paragraph long, and no help at all. Dinah knew that Mr. Dixon expected them to quote facts and figures in the debate. He didn't just want opinions.

Dinah was ready to give up and go across the street to Mrs. Briscoe's house for a study break. But then the librarian helping her in the grown-up part of the library made a suggestion. "Have you tried the microfiche catalog?" he asked. "You may find a book on this topic that would be equivalent to a dozen articles."

It was worth a try. The man helped Dinah find the right page in the microfiche. She scanned down the long column of type—California, canning, capital gains tax . . . capital punishment! There *was* a whole book on capital punishment: *Capital Punishment: For and Against*, by William MacGregor. And when Dinah danced over to check the shelves, there it was, waiting for her, ready to be checked out.

The book was perfect. As Dinah skimmed through it, she could tell it was a debater's dream. It gave every argument for capital punishment and every argument against, each complete with relevant Supreme Court cases and quotes from famous people who had spoken on the subject.

"I just won the debate," Dinah whispered to Suzanne, back at their table near the window. She held the book so that Suzanne could see. "It's all here. Everything. Nick Tribble, prepare to meet thy doom!"

"Poor Nick," Suzanne said. "He really doesn't have a chance now."

"Su-zanne! Whose side are you on?"

"Yours. It's just . . . Nick will never find anything as good as that."

"So why didn't he come to the library? It's a public library. I'll tell you why. He was too busy hiding in my bushes singing about how my hair is frizzy."

"You're right," Suzanne said. "And if he had found it first, he probably wouldn't have shared it with you."

"Probably? Definitely." Dinah fished in her backpack for her library card. She had no obligation to share the book with Nick, none at all. If Nick had wanted her to share her library book with him, he shouldn't have thrown that bra at her head. Or tried out for her part in the play. Or burped in her face during the audition. Or ruined her first baby-sitting job.

"Isn't there some saying about how everything is fair in war?" Dinah asked Suzanne.

"'All's fair in love and war,'" Suzanne quoted.

"Well," said Dinah. She hadn't remembered the love part. "All right then. This is war."

Sunday night Dinah found time to work on publicity for the dance. She wrote a musical morning announcement, to be sung to the tune of "America the Beautiful":

> Oh, beautiful, for growing trees
> That will not be chopped down
> To make a bunch of math work sheets
> That cause us all to frown.
> Recycling, recycling!
> Oh, would this waste would stop!
> If you would like to do your part,
> Then come to our sock hop!

Dinah wished she could sing it on the morning announcements herself. Too bad she couldn't carry a tune. At least her turn at morning announcements was coming up, on the very week of the dance, too. By then she could probably think of some even better publicity.

Before she went to bed, Dinah finished two dozen posters. On each she drew two pairs of dancing socks, which she colored with electrifyingly bright markers. Underneath she printed the caption: WHO ARE YOU INVITING TO THE SOCK HOP?

This was clearly the question of the month for the sixth-grade girls at John F. Kennedy Middle School. The girls at Dinah's lunch table talked about nothing else. Suzanne had already invited Greg, naturally. Blaine had narrowed her choice down to either John Carlucci, the class treasurer, or Amory Cruz, who played on the boys' soccer team. Mandy Bricker from Drama Club, Dinah's other competition for the part of Olivia, was going to invite a seventh grader from another school.

Dinah still insisted that she wasn't inviting anybody. But it was beginning to seem as if she were the only sixth-grade girl who wasn't.

"You have to invite *somebody*," Mandy said at lunch on Monday.

Blaine agreed. "You're practically running the dance. It'll look too strange if you don't even go to it."

"I'm going to go. I'm just not going to ask anybody."

"Why not?" Blaine wanted to know.

"Because." It was too hard to explain.

"'Because' isn't a reason," Blaine said.

"Just ask Nick and be done with it," Suzanne advised. "He obviously expects you to."

"The reason I don't ask Nick," Dinah explained, "is because I would rather die." At least she knew the answer there.

"Ask someone else then," Mandy said.

"Like who?"

"Like anyone who isn't Nick," Blaine said.

Maybe Dinah should, after all. Maybe if she asked

someone else to the dance, Nick would stop hiding in her bushes and making up songs in her honor. It wouldn't count as asking a boy to a dance if you were only doing it to avoid asking a certain other boy.

The trouble was that Dinah didn't really like boys. And boys didn't really like Dinah. Invite anyone who isn't Nick, Blaine had said. Dinah was attracted to that idea. But which anyone? Which boy who wasn't Nick should it be?

There was Artie Adams. Dinah had known Artie since second grade, from her classes each year at Riverdale Elementary. You might say that Artie was an old friend. But it would be more accurate to say that Artie was an old enemy. The time in fifth grade that Dinah had climbed out the classroom window and danced on the school roof in the rain, it had been Artie Adams who'd shut the window so that she couldn't get back inside before the substitute teacher returned and sent her to the principal's office. Still, Artie was funny, and Dinah was used to him by now.

There was Jason Winfield. Last fall Jason and Dinah had both run against Blaine for the office of sixth-grade class president. Dinah had run on a recycling platform, promising to start a schoolwide recycling program if she was elected. It had been Jason Winfield who had given Dinah the nickname of Bucket Head because she wore her family's big yellow recycling bucket to school on her head, as a campaign publicity stunt. In the end, Dinah had withdrawn from the race in Blaine's favor, to make sure that she and Blaine didn't split the girls' votes and cause Jason to win. So Jason had no particular reason to be fond of Dinah. Still, he was handsome and athletic, and a lot of girls liked him. Maybe Dinah should, too.

The only other choices were Todd Burstyn or Paul Hatfield from Drama Club. Paul already had a girl-friend, but Todd didn't. Todd was quiet and serious compared to Dinah, but people said opposites were supposed to attract.

Was Nick an opposite to Dinah or the same as Dinah? More the same, really, Dinah had to admit, in a gross boy version. Dinah liked attention; Nick did, too. Nick and Dinah both had a flair for the humorous and the dramatic. If opposites attracted, sames repelled. That much seemed right, at least in this case.

By the end of eighth period, Dinah was in a frenzy of mingled anticipation and dread. Mrs. Bevens was going to post the cast list for *Love Saves the Day* directly after school, on the bulletin board next to the Drama Club room.

What if Nick was Wilfredo, Suzanne was Olivia, and Dinah was *nothing*?

What if Dinah and Suzanne were *both* nothing?

What if Nick was Manly and Dinah was Olivia and they had to kiss—really kiss—during every single rehearsal?

"You look for me," Dinah told Suzanne, clutching Suzanne's hand as they approached the small crowd of sixth graders gathered in front of the bulletin board.

Dinah shut her eyes and waited.

Suzanne gave a squeal of delight. "You're Wilfredo! And I'm Olivia!"

Eyes wide open now, Dinah elbowed her way to the front of the group. Sure enough, the cast list read:

Manly Allweather ...... Todd Burstyn
Olivia Montpelier ...... Suzanne Kelly
Wilfredo Desperado ...... Dinah Seabrooke
Mrs. Montpelier ...... Mandy Bricker
Humphrey Montpelier ...... Paul Hatfield
Gypsy Fortune-teller ...... Heather Allen

Dinah read the whole cast list twice before she realized that Nick's name wasn't on it. Then she saw it at the very bottom of the page, under "Backstage Crew."

Mrs. Bevens must have been really mad about Nick's burp. And it had been a juvenile and disgusting thing to do. Still, it seemed unfair to Dinah that Nick should come away from the tryouts with no part at all. He was a better actor than Todd and Paul put together. He would have made as good a Wilfredo as Dinah herself. Now that the part was hers, Dinah didn't mind admitting this.

Dinah didn't see Nick in the group next to the bulletin board. Hadn't he even bothered to check the list? Or had he been there already and then slipped away to hide his disappointment?

It was a strange thought that Nick Tribble might have *feelings*.

7

Rehearsals for *Love Saves the Day* began after school on Tuesday, and Dinah threw herself into her hard-won role with gusto. It had been over a year since she had been in a play. She had almost forgotten how much fun acting was. The backstage crew wasn't coming to rehearsals the first week, so rehearsals were pleasantly burp-free.

Even though the rest of the cast wouldn't wear costumes and makeup until the final dress rehearsal, Mrs. Bevens had Dinah wear her long-handled black mustache from the start. Dinah looked perfectly dashing in it, and by the end of the week she could twirl it with an expert cackle.

"I was born to play Wilfredo," Dinah told Suzanne, as they rode the bus home together on Friday afternoon. "And you were born to play Olivia."

Even better than a starring role in the class play was a starring role for you and one for your best friend, too. And none for Nick Tribble. Dinah had gotten over her first twinge of sorriness for Nick. She had expected him to say something to her Tuesday morning in home-room—to congratulate her, or tease her, or *something*. Instead he had given another gigantic burp, one so loud and obnoxious that Mrs. Vogel had given him two days' detention for it.

On Saturday morning, Dinah recited Wilfredo's lines for her parents at breakfast. They hissed and booed in all the right places, which made Benjamin squeal with delight. Then Dinah's father got ready to go to the store.

"Today's the big spring sale," he said. "We're going to be busy all day, that's for sure."

"Can I come help?" Dinah asked.

"Not today," her father said. "There's going to be too much commotion there already."

"I won't make commotion. I promise. You won't even know I'm there except that I'll straighten all the tables for you when they get messed up."

Her father exchanged looks with her mother.

"Really," Dinah said. "I'll be the Employee of the Week. I'll be the Invisible Helper. I'll be the world-famous Table Straightener."

"Something tells me I'm making a big mistake," her father said, "but, all right, you may come. But, Dinah, no high jinks in the store windows. And no horseplay in the aisles with the boys."

Dinah drew herself up with wounded dignity. "Believe me," she said. "I have no intention of *horseplay* in the aisles with *boys*."

Dinah hardly knew why she wanted to go to the

store so much. But she loved sale days, she really did. The hustle and bustle of the bargain-hunting crowd always put Dinah in a cheerful mood. And you never knew who might come into the store on sale days. It might be—just anybody. Just anybody at all.

The store opened at 9:30 on Saturdays. By 9:15 that morning, several shoppers had already gathered outside to be the first in line for the early-bird specials. True to her word, Dinah didn't clown around, but went straight to work helping her father's three assistants wheel out racks of sale merchandise from the back. She picked up a tennis racket that had strayed into the golf display. She tidied up the women's bathing suits. She dusted the soccer balls.

Then it was 9:30. Her father unlocked the front doors, and the waiting throng of customers swept in. The spring sale had begun.

The first person Dinah saw whom she knew was Mr. Prensky, her English teacher from school. At school Mr. Prensky never seemed to like Dinah very much. He claimed she was "disruptive" in class, which on occasion in the past had been true. But now, without his jacket and bow tie, he looked like a different man. Dinah almost didn't recognize him without his copy of *Fun with Grammar*.

"Why, it's Dinah Seabrooke!" he greeted her, as if she were his long-lost friend. He gave a puzzled look at the red jersey Dinah wore to mark her as a member of the sales staff. "Aren't you a bit young for a job like this?"

"My father's the manager," Dinah explained.

"In that case, perhaps you could direct me to the cycling wear," Mr. Prensky said. "I need some new cycling shorts."

Mr. Prensky in cycling shorts! But Dinah didn't fall on the floor, screaming with hysterical laughter. "Cycling things are by the back wall, next to the dressing room." She pointed politely.

Who else in the sixth grade would have been as mature and responsible in such an instance? Certainly not Nick Tribble.

Mandy Bricker came in with her parents to try on swimsuits.

"Remember that seventh grader I was going to ask to the dance?" Mandy asked Dinah when she saw her. "Well, I did, and he said—yes!"

Dinah didn't say, Who cares? Instead she said, "That's nice."

"Did you ask anyone yet?" Mandy asked.

"Nope."

"I think Katie Richards is on the brink of asking Nick Tribble."

"She can have him."

"You'd better hurry up, Dinah," Mandy advised. "This is the week. The boys are going fast."

"I believe dressing room number two is ready now," Dinah replied.

And Mandy floated off, swimsuits in hand, never guessing that in that very dressing room half an hour ago, Mr. Prensky had been trying on skintight Lycra cycling shorts.

Over the next hour Dinah saw more kids from school, and Suzanne's social studies teacher, and the Harmons from next door. She dazzled each one in turn with her courteous professionalism.

Then, at 11:15, who should walk into the store but Nick Tribble and Artie Adams. As soon as Dinah saw Nick, she realized that she had been expecting him all along. "Lightning never strikes twice," people said. But another saying, just as fitting, was: "A criminal always returns to the scene of the crime."

"Ocean-River!"

Nick and Artie came up to Dinah as she was straightening the swimsuit rack for the tenth time. "How come you're not in the window? I told young Irving Arthur here that you would be."

"I can't talk now," Dinah said "I'm working."

"Aw, come on, Dinah," Artie said. "Climb in the window just for a minute. I want to throw a bra on your head."

"Get lost," Dinah said. Then she remembered: Never offend a customer. Were Nick and Artie customers? Dinah doubted it. But she forced herself to be more polite, anyway. "I mean, may I help you? Are you looking for anything in particular this morning or are you just browsing?"

"I'm looking for bras," Artie said. "Great big ones."

If Artie didn't watch out, Dinah would throw a bra at *his* head. But that might count as horseplay in the aisle with boys.

"I'm looking for socks," Nick said. "To wear to the sock hop. In case anybody asks me."

He grinned, and Dinah felt oddly tempted to ask him on the spot. She stopped herself in time and pointed to the rack of socks next to the athletic shoes.

"Come with us," Nick said. "We need some help picking them out."

"I can't," Dinah said. But she probably *should* check to see if the sock rack needed straightening.

It did, badly. Customers were messy. Even people who were neat at home became slobs once they walked into a store.

"Look at these, Dinah," Nick said. He held up a pair of fluffy brown socks. "Maybe I should get them. They match your frizzy hair."

"They do not," Dinah said. "Besides, my hair isn't frizzy, it's curly."

"If I put one of these frizz socks on a baseball, it would look just like you," Nick said. "Did anyone ever tell you your head looks like a baseball with a frizzy sock on it?"

"If you're not going to buy anything, why don't you just leave?" Dinah asked him.

"Who said I'm not going to buy anything? I'm going to buy these socks, so we'll match at the dance—your frizzy head and my frizzy feet."

"Forget it," Dinah said. "I wouldn't ask you to the dance if you were the last boy on earth. I'd rather ask Count Dracula than ask you. I'd rather ask—*Artie*."

Artie looked up from the sock sale bin, alarmed.

Dinah was alarmed herself, but it was too late to turn back. The fateful words had been spoken. As half a dozen other customers stood watching in the sudden silence that descended on the sock section, Dinah turned to Artie. She spoke slowly and distinctly so that there could be no mistaking the question.

"I, Dinah Marie Seabrooke, hereby ask you, Irving Arthur Adams, to the sixth-grade sock hop. Will you go with me?"

With a green sock on one hand and a blue-and-white striped sock on the other, Artie advanced toward her.

He couldn't very well say no, could he? Didn't you have to go to a dance with the first person who asked you? At least that was the mannerly thing to do. But was Artie a mannerly person? Still, he wouldn't refuse in front of six other sock buyers.

"I, Irving Arthur Adams, hereby reply to Dinah Marie Seabrooke . . ."

Dinah stood waiting. Nick stood waiting. The six other customers stood waiting.

"No!"

No?

Dinah didn't know if she was relieved or angry. Now she wouldn't have to go to the dance with Artie. That was the good part. But it was humiliating to be turned down point-blank, by Artie of all people, in front of an audience. She felt her cheeks burning. She felt like strangling Artie with a pair of striped exercise tights, and then strangling Nick, too, for good measure.

Horseplay in the aisles with boys was turning out to be practically irresistible.

"I turned Dinah do-own. I turned Dinah do-own."

"I was just *joking*," Dinah said, as scornfully as she could. "Don't you know a joke when you hear one?"

But if Artie had said yes, she would have gone to the dance with him. So Dinah knew it was only half a joke. She couldn't let herself look at Nick. Somehow, once again, disaster had overtaken her, and somehow, once again, it seemed all Nick's fault.

8

"Do you know if anyone has asked Jason Winfield to the dance?" Dinah asked the other girls casually at lunch on Monday. She hadn't told anyone except Suzanne about her rejected invitation to Artie.

"I don't think so," Blaine said. "But someone's sure to soon. He's awfully good-looking."

"If you like that type," Dinah put in quickly.

"What type?" Suzanne asked.

"You know. The jock type. The big-muscle type."

"Who *doesn't* like that type?" Mandy asked. "I thought about asking him myself. But it's more exciting to go with a seventh grader."

That afternoon, in sixth-period social studies, Dinah studied Jason more closely. He was brawny for a sixth grader. It would be easy to mistake him for an older boy, a seventh or even an eighth grader. Dinah had attended a couple of the home baseball games, and Jason was already one of the team's stars. He could hit a pitched baseball deep into center field. He could catch a ball with an easy stretch of his mitt. Better a boy who threw baseballs than a boy who threw bras.

The only drawback was that Jason was a jerk. He had opposed the school's recycling program, which both Blaine and Dinah had supported. He didn't mind cutting down trees to make math work sheets. He thought that was what trees were *for*. So it would be strange to invite Jason to the sock hop, a dance whose sole purpose was to raise money for recycling.

But you couldn't not ask a boy to a dance just because he was a jerk. As Mandy had said, boys were going fast. Even Nick was likely to get an invitation soon, from Katie.

So Jason it would be. But this time Dinah wasn't going to ask a boy in public. Her face still flamed when she remembered Artie's booming "No!" This time Dinah would ask in private. Better still, she would send a note.

Dinah worked on her note all evening. She felt like reading it over the phone to Suzanne, but after she had dialed Suzanne's number, she hung up before the phone had a chance to ring. Some things were too embarrassing to tell even your best friend. So she read her invitation over to herself one last time instead.

Dear Jason,

As you know, the sixth-grade sock hop is two weeks away. Girls are supposed to ask boys. So I'm asking you.

Don't worry. This doesn't mean I like you. As a boy, that is. But I decided to ask somebody, and I figured it might as well be you.

I know you opposed recycling in the election last fall, but by now you've probably seen the error of your ways. I hope you're big enough to admit that you were wrong, and Blaine and I were right.

Anyway, do you want to go to the dance with me or not?

> Sincerely,
> Dinah Seabrooke
> R.S.V.P.

R.S.V.P. was French for "Please write back." Dinah hoped Jason would write back right away. A simple yes or no would suffice.

In homeroom the next morning, Dinah took the note out of her grammar book and folded it into a small, plump triangle, neatly tucking in every corner. It looked like a bullet, or an Indian arrowhead—so small, and yet so lethal.

Then, when she was sure Nick wasn't looking, she carefully placed the note on the corner of Jason's desk. Jason picked it up and put it into his shirt pocket.

Instantly, Dinah began to wish she had her note back. What if Jason said yes, and she had to go to the dance with him? What if he said no, and she had to face a second humiliation? What if he showed her note to the other boys? What if he showed it to Nick?

Dinah thought about writing a second note:

Dear Jason,
    Please ignore my first note.
    I take back everything in it.

> Sincerely,
> Dinah Seabrooke

Or maybe she could just ask Jason to give her the first note back. Excuse me, Jason, I believe I dropped a note on your desk by mistake. But she had printed his name so plainly on the front of the folded triangle.

Dinah tried to remember what the note had said. She had only read it over fifty times the night before. She *had* been quite clear that she didn't like Jason, hadn't she? Or might he think that she had just *said* she didn't like him, but actually *did* like him? Why else, after all, would a girl invite a boy to a dance? "Actions speak louder than words," Dinah's father always said.

If he did think she liked him, what then? Would that make him more likely to go to the dance with her, or less? And why didn't he open the note and *read* it?

"What's the matter, Dinah?" Blaine asked her as they walked to first-period English together. "You seem jumpy this morning."

Dinah jumped when Blaine said it. "Jumpy? Me? No, I'm not jumpy."

"Well, it's all settled," Blaine said. "I asked Amory Cruz to the dance, and he said he'd go with me."

"How did you ask him? Did you just go up to him and ask, or did you send him a note?"

"I just asked him. One time when nobody else was around. I'd never ask a boy something like that in a note."

"Oh," Dinah said. "Why not?"

"For one thing, I wouldn't want it to fall into the wrong hands. And what if he never wrote back? You know how boys are. If you ask them something face to face, they have to answer. But with a note, you might never hear back from them, either way."

Those were good reasons not to invite a boy to a dance by a note, all right.

Dinah saw Jason in science class third period. He didn't say anything to her about the note. Had he read it yet? But in fourth-period math class she saw him showing a folded piece of paper to Nick. Both boys were laughing.

On the way to lunch Dinah told Suzanne what she had done.

"A note?"

Dinah could tell Suzanne was stalling to give herself time to think of something comforting to say.

"I guess— I mean, I guess if you had asked me, I would have said not to send a note, but I'm not sure that a note is *such* a terrible thing. But I didn't know you liked Jason, Dinah."

"I *don't*," Dinah wailed. "I don't like Artie, either. I just like them better than—"

"Nick," Suzanne finished for her. "You're too much, Dinah. Just do me a favor. When you ask Nick to the dance, don't do it by a note, okay?"

"Don't worry," Dinah told her. "After this, I'm never asking a boy to a dance ever again."

By social studies sixth period, Dinah could stand the suspense no longer. Should she send Jason a note demanding to know if he had read her first note? Not that she had gotten anywhere with her first note, but maybe when it came to sending notes to boys, two wrongs made a right. Or something like that. She could send him a note with two little boxes on it, one marked yes and one marked no.

Dinah took a piece of notebook paper out of her three-ring binder and began to write.

Dear Jason,
    Don't you know what RSVP means? It means: Write back!
    If you don't want to go to the dance with me, fine! But I have to know by the end of sixth period today. So that I can ask someone more worthy of the honor.
    Please check the box with your answer:
    ☐ Yes.
    ☐ No.

                    Sincerely,
                    Dinah Seabrooke

Dinah folded the note into a second bullet. As soon as Mr. Dixon turned to the chalkboard, she tossed the bullet smack into the middle of Jason's desk.

To her relief, this time he opened it right away. As Dinah watched, he took his pen and checked one of the boxes. Which one? But instead of folding the note back into its triangle, he refolded it into a paper airplane.

Mr. Dixon turned to write something else on the board. Jason flew the airplane back in the direction of Dinah's desk. Unfortunately Mr. Dixon whirled around as it was in midflight.

"Winfield! This isn't a landing strip! Bring that airplane here to me."

A slight wind current in the room sent the airplane to the floor two desks from Dinah's. Before Dinah could leap out of her seat and pounce on it, Mr. Dixon had scooped it up. He glanced at it briefly.

"Ahem," he said. "This appears to be an important message from Winfield to Seabrooke. You may collect it from me after class, Seabrooke." And he laid the paper airplane in the middle of his desk as the rest of the class tittered.

Dinah was furious. Mr. Dixon had no right to read somebody else's mail. Of course, he had thought he was just reading somebody else's airplane. At least he hadn't read it out loud. But still, now everyone in the class knew that Jason had sent a note to Dinah. Everyone, including Nick.

Yes or no? No or yes? Dinah would have to wait another half hour to find out.

Suddenly Mr. Dixon whirled around from the board a second time. "*More* airplanes!" he bellowed. "What is this, Dulles International Airport? Richards, bring that airplane to me."

Dinah turned around in her seat to see Katie Richards, near tears, clutching a paper airplane in her hand. Who was *her* airplane from? Katie sat next to Nick. What did *her* airplane say?

"Richards! Here, on my desk."

Slowly Katie brought her airplane forward. Mr. Dixon scanned it the same way he had Dinah's.

"This appears to be an important message from

Tribble to Richards. You may collect it from me after class, Richards. But the next airplane I see will get its pilot two weeks' detention." Mr. Dixon rapped the chalkboard twice, for emphasis. "Two weeks. Is that clear?"

Somehow the period drew to a close. At last the bell rang. Dinah and Katie went together to the front of the room to collect their airplanes.

"Let me make sure you each get the right one," Mr. Dixon said merrily. "All right, Seabrooke, one for *you*; and Richards, one for *you*."

Dinah waited until she was in the hall to look at hers. Some people liked to read their paper airplanes in private. One glance told her all she needed to know. Jason had scrawled a big black X in the box for no.

Behind her, Katie gave a shriek. "He said yes! Nick said yes!"

Yes to what? But Dinah already knew.

9

Dinah had to get *someone* to go to the dance with her. She just had to.

During play rehearsal that afternoon, she studied Todd Burstyn. He was really as nice looking as Jason or Nick. Only he was quieter, so that girls didn't notice him much. And he was shorter than Dinah, by an inch or so. But when he recited Manly's lines he sounded quite—manly. When he had to kiss Suzanne during rehearsal, he just kissed her, quickly, shyly, the way a hero was supposed to do.

This time Dinah wasn't going to ask a boy in public *or* by a note. This time she was going to make sure the boy liked her first. Did Todd like her? He didn't *dislike* her, so she was off to a better start with him already. Today was Tuesday. She'd ask Todd on Friday, at the latest. That gave her three days to get him to fall in love with her. Or at least, to fall in like.

"Hi, Todd." Dinah sat down next to him as Suzanne rehearsed a scene with Paul, who played her young ward, and Mandy, who played her mother.

Todd looked surprised at the greeting. Hadn't anyone ever said hi to him before? In America, people said hi all the time.

"Hi," Todd said, after a longish pause.

So far, so good.

"Do you think we'll be ready to perform the play by the assembly next week?" Dinah asked him.

Todd nodded.

"Do you know all your lines?" Dinah asked.

Todd nodded again.

"I know mine, too. Paul still forgets some of his, though."

No comment from Todd.

"Maybe you could help him practice. Are you two best friends?"

"Uh-huh."

"Suzanne and I are best friends. Do you and Paul have a special food you like to eat together? Suzanne and I like to eat M&M's. She likes the brown ones best, and I like the red ones. Until Suzanne, I never knew anyone who actually liked brown M&M's. I mean, do you?"

"Do I what?"

"Like brown M&M's? Or know anybody who does?"

Todd shrugged.

"All right, Manly, Wilfredo," Mrs. Bevens called. "We need you up here for the next scene."

So much for Dinah's first attempt at conversation with Todd.

That night at dinner, Dinah asked her parents, "How do you get a boy to talk to you?"

"If it's that Nick, the less he says, the better," Dinah's mother said.

"It isn't Nick."

Dinah's father looked up. "It isn't Nick? Who is it, then?"

"Todd. He's Manly in the play. I might—well, I'm not sure I'm going to ask him to the dance, but I might."

Dinah had never told her parents about her invitations to Artie and Jason.

"But what about Nick?" her father asked.

"I wouldn't ask him if you paid me a million dollars. Besides, he's going with somebody else. With Katie Richards. So I might ask Todd. But I can't get him to say more than three words to me."

"That reminds me of a story I once heard about President Calvin Coolidge," Dinah's father said. "Silent Cal, he was called. A talkative lady sat next to him at a White House dinner, and cooed in his ear, 'Mr. President, I made a bet before I came that I can get you to say more than two words.' Mr. Coolidge turned to her and said, 'You lose,' and those were the only words he spoke to her for the rest of the evening."

"And he didn't end up marrying her later, or anything like that?"

"Nope," her father said. "At least not that I ever heard of."

Well, Silent Todd didn't have to marry Dinah. He

just had to go to the sock hop with her. So what if he didn't talk much? Dinah was perfectly capable of talking for two.

"Do you think Todd likes me?" Dinah asked Suzanne on the bus the next morning.

"Sure," Suzanne said. "He likes you. Or do you mean, '*likes* you' likes you?"

"Well, sort of. I mean, likes me enough to go to the dance with me."

Suzanne looked worried then. "I don't think Todd—though I guess he *might*—it's not like he likes anyone *else*—but I still don't think he—"

"If I want to get him to like me by Friday, what should I do?"

"By Friday? Like in two days?" Suzanne thought for a minute. "Just talk to him, I guess. Take an interest in things that interest him. It might not hurt to let him know that you like *him*. But not so much as to scare him off."

"How do you let a boy know you like him?"

"You know. Just act friendly, talk to him, listen when he talks to you."

"I already did that, and it didn't work. Is there any other way?"

"There're a hundred other ways. You can write his name in a heart on the cover of your book and leave it somewhere where he'll see it. Or you can walk by his house some afternoon and then act surprised if you see him out in his yard and say, 'I didn't know *you* lived here.' Or you can call him on the telephone, and when he answers, pretend you got the wrong number."

How did Suzanne know all these things? Suzanne, Dinah's own best friend.

"And if he starts to like me, what will *he* do? How will I know?"

"He'll hide in your bushes and sing insulting songs," Suzanne said matter-of-factly. "And if he really likes you, he'll throw a bra at your head."

Dinah figured she could try decorating the covers of her textbooks.

D.S. + T.B. she wrote on the cover of *Fun with Grammar* during homeroom. She drew lacy hearts with Todd's name in them on the cover of *New Approaches to Math*. And on the cover of *Exploring Our World: A Basic Sixth-Grade Science Text*, she wrote DINAH LOVES TODD FOREVER AND EVER.

Suzanne's eyes widened when she saw them first period. "I was thinking of one little heart," she said.

"I guess I got carried away," Dinah admitted. "But I don't have all year. I have to speed things up a little bit."

Todd was in three of Dinah's classes, but he didn't sit close enough to her to see the covers of her textbooks. Nick saw them, though.

"D. S. + T. B.?" he asked, as they filed into social studies sixth period. "Don't you mean D. S. + N. T.?"

"Don't *you* mean N. T. + K. R.?" Dinah shot back.

"I mean, N. T. + F. H.," Nick said.

"Who's F. H.?" Dinah shouldn't have asked, but she did.

"Frizz Head. Who's T. B.?"

"N. O. Y. B."

"Okay, D. O. R.," Nick said.

"What kind of crazy code is that?" Jason asked Nick. "You and Bucket Head sound like talking robots."

It was all too complicated for Dinah. Jason called her Bucket Head, and he plainly didn't like her; at least he didn't "*like* her" like her. But when Nick called her Frizz Head, Suzanne acted as if Nick *did* "like her" like her. Bucket Head and Frizz Head sounded the same to Dinah. She wished she were back in fifth grade, before there were horrible dances where girls asked boys.

Before rehearsal, Dinah spread out her books on the edge of the stage at the front of the auditorium. Anyone whose name was Todd or whose initials were T. B. would be bound to have a jolt of surprise on seeing them.

Except for Todd Burstyn.

"Are these yours?" he asked Dinah, picking them up to get them out of the way.

"Mine?" Dinah asked. "Is my name on them?"

Todd looked. "Yes," he said.

And your name? Isn't your name on them, too? But there was nothing for Dinah to do but go to the stage and collect her books, decorated covers and all.

So much for Wednesday.

On Thursday Suzanne stayed at home, sick with the

twenty-four-hour stomach flu. Mrs. Bevens looked distressed when Dinah told her.

"Oh, Dinah, with our schedule so tight, we can't lose a day's rehearsal. Here, take off your mustache, dear, and read Suzanne's lines in her scenes with Todd."

Dinah had a sudden thought. Maybe her mustache had been part of the problem. Maybe Todd had trouble getting romantically interested in a girl with a long-handled black mustache.

Dinah had seen movies on TV in which at some point the hero tenderly takes off the heroine's eyeglasses and pulls the hairpins out of her prim bun, and when her long hair comes tumbling down and she looks at him for the first time without her glasses on, he sees how beautiful she is, and they kiss. It might work the same if the hero tenderly removed the heroine's bushy black fake mustache.

Was she just imagining it, or was Todd looking at her with new eyes as she faced him now, for the first time with no mustache, playing Olivia to his Manly?

They rehearsed the scene where Manly comes upon Olivia tied to a tree—by Wilfredo—in the front yard of her family farmhouse, with a raging forest fire coming ever closer. Manly frees her, and they fight the fire together.

Then: "Oh, Manly," Dinah said. She didn't need her script for these lines. There was no danger that she would forget them, ever.

"Yes, my dear?" Todd as Manly replied.

Dinah raised her downcast eyes and looked at Todd.

"You—you saved my farm. You saved my honor. You saved . . . my life. How can I ever thank you?"

"I did not do it for your thanks."

"Then, why? You risked all for me. I must give you something in return."

"I ask only . . . your love."

"If you want so poor a thing, it is yours!"

Todd took Dinah in his arms and kissed her. It was over before Dinah had a chance to get ready for it. Still, it had been a real kiss, on the mouth, or at least near the mouth. Dinah's first kiss. She wished she could remember more about it.

"Todd, dear, don't pause quite so long on that last line," Mrs. Bevens called from her seat in the middle of the auditorium. "We don't want the audience to think the play is over halfway through your best line. Try it again."

"I ask only your love."

Todd took Dinah in his arms and kissed her again. This time Dinah felt the pressure of Todd's lips against hers, however briefly.

"But do pause a *little* bit, Todd, dear. We want just a moment of hesitation before those last thrilling words are uttered."

"I ask only . . . your love."

Kiss number three. Kissing Todd was a bit like kissing a windup kissing doll. The doll would say a line in a mechanical doll's voice—sometimes faster, sometimes slower, depending on how tightly he had been wound. And then, with jerky, mechanical motions—sometimes faster, sometimes slower—the doll would execute its kiss. Talk. Kiss. Talk. Kiss. Talk. Kiss.

Still, it was hard not to feel *something* for a boy who had just kissed you three times. Todd must have felt something, too.

"All right, Todd, Dinah. That's enough for now," Mrs. Bevens said.

Overcome by the intensity of the moment, Dinah whispered to Todd in her best Olivia voice: "Will you go to the sock hop with me?"

Yes, my dear; if you want so poor a thing, it is yours!

"Sock hop?" Todd asked. "What's a sock hop?"

Dinah felt as if she had come upon one of those kids from a survey on how ignorant American students are—the kind who can't find the United States on a map of North America and don't know the president's name. How could Todd go to JFK Middle School and not know about the recycling sock hop? Hadn't he seen any of Dinah's two dozen posters with the dancing socks: WHO ARE *YOU* INVITING TO THE SOCK HOP? Didn't he listen to morning announcements? Didn't the boys at his cafeteria table spend the whole lunch period every day talking about which girls they hoped would ask them?

"It's a dance," Dinah said. "To raise money for the recycling program. It's on Friday, May tenth. Girls are supposed to ask boys." And I just asked you.

"Let's back up a bit," Mrs. Bevens said. "Dinah, dear, put your mustache back on, and Mandy, dear, you be our Olivia for a while. I want to hear the scene where Wilfredo tells Olivia that if she won't marry him he'll foreclose the mortgage on her farm."

Dinah climbed down from the stage and stuck her mustache back on. She did her usual good job in her scene as Wilfredo, but when she was done, she took the mustache off again. She really did feel prettier without it.

Another scene with Mandy as Olivia, and rehearsal was over. Todd still hadn't given his reply.

"So?" Dinah asked him as they headed down the hall toward the bus.

Todd looked wretched. But he didn't have to say more than one little word: yes or no. If that was too much, he could nod or shake his head.

"Yes or no?" Dinah asked, to help him out.

"Oh, Dinah," Todd said. "I don't want to hurt your feelings or anything. I think you're really great in the play. But I don't want to go to a dance. I don't know anything about dancing. Maybe in high school I'll go to dances, if I have to, but this one is only two weeks away. So, if you don't mind very much, well, I'd rather not."

This torrent of words from Silent Todd put Dinah at a loss for words herself.

Me, too! she wanted to shout. I don't want to go, either!

"That's okay," Dinah told Todd.

His face brightened. "Really?"

"Really."

At least Dinah had gotten Todd to say more than two words. It was a victory of sorts. But now *three* boys had turned down her invitation to the dance. Strike one, Artie; strike two, Jason; strike three, Todd.

Dinah wasn't a baseball fan, but she knew about strikes: three of them, and you're out.

10

"You could ask someone else," Suzanne suggested doubtfully on the phone that evening, after Dinah had reported on the day's events.

"Are you kidding?" Dinah asked. "They'd put me in the *Guinness Book of World Records* if four boys turned me down. World's most unpopular girl. Something like that."

Actually, Dinah had always wanted to be in the *Guinness Book of World Records*. But not for this. Not for something embarrassing and . . . depressing, really. The first rejection hadn't depressed her, or the second. They had just made her mad and more determined to forge ahead with her goal. But with the third, rejection was starting to sting.

Dinah had almost forgotten what her original goal was supposed to be. To not ask Nick to the dance? There had to be an easier way of not asking one boy than asking three others who each rejected you in turn.

"You're not unpopular," Suzanne said.

"*Three* rejections?"

"Look, you asked the wrong boys, and you asked them the wrong way. Artie? *Jason?* You don't even like them. And you asked them in the most insulting way possible. 'I'd rather go with a snake. I'd rather go with Artie.' Or rubbing it in to Jason that he lost the election. Todd wasn't such a bad idea, and at least you didn't put him down or anything, but you can tell from a mile away that Todd isn't interested in girls or dances."

"None of the rest of you got *any* rejections."

"You wouldn't have, either, if you had asked Nick. You knew from the start that it was your destiny to go with Nick. But you didn't listen to your destiny."

"Ha! I knew from the start that it was my destiny to go alone. And I *am* going alone. So I was right all along."

"Besides," Suzanne went on, as if Dinah hadn't spoken, "how do you think Nick feels about all this? Talk about rejection. He gave you about four million hints that he wanted you to ask him, and all you did was ask other people right in front of him."

"What hints? Throwing a bra at me? Burping in my face? Singing songs about my frizzy hair?" Though Dinah suddenly remembered Nick at the spring sale, saying he needed to buy some socks for the dance "in case anybody asks me." Had she hurt Nick's feelings? Did Nick *have* feelings? Dinah had asked herself the same thing after Mrs. Bevens posted the cast list for the play. But even if Nick did have feelings, surely he didn't have feelings the way she, Dinah, had feelings.

"Anyway," Dinah said, "he's going with Katie. He sure didn't reject *her* invitation." It was time to change the subject. "Are you going to be in school tomorrow?"

"I think so. I have to, with the play just a week away."

"Those three kisses from Todd today?" Dinah was back on the same subject in spite of herself. "They're probably the only kisses I'll ever get in my life. I've decided I'm never getting married. I'm going to be a— What's the word for a woman who never gets married?"

"An old maid?"

"No, the other word."

"A spinster."

Dinah liked the sound of it.

"I'm going to be a spinster. Kings and princes and emperors will come from far and wide to beg me to go to sock hops with them, but I'll turn them all down and work on my career as a great actress and debater."

"If you say so," Suzanne said, apparently too weak from her flu to argue any further. It was actually a relief to have this settled. Dinah had tried boys, she had tried romance, and it hadn't worked out. Now that she knew this she could concentrate her energies elsewhere. Very few eleven-year-olds were lucky enough to know that lifelong spinsterhood lay before them.

And yet there was an odd lump in Dinah's throat after she finished talking with Suzanne. The sock hop was the first of all the dances that were to come in middle school, in high school, in college, and beyond. Suzanne's older brother, Tom, was taking a girl to the high-school prom. Dinah's parents went out dancing sometimes. Mrs. Briscoe had danced with Mr. Briscoe. Was everyone dancing except Dinah? Of course, a person could always dance alone. Dinah had danced alone that time on the school roof in the rain, back in fifth grade. But would it be fun to dance with someone else? With a boy you liked? A boy who liked you?

But there was no boy Dinah liked who liked her. Unless—*did* she like Nick? *Did* he like her? If so, they were both showing it in odd ways. What if Dinah had asked Nick to the dance? It seemed to Dinah that if she had asked Nick and he had said yes, then she would be like all the other girls at her lunchroom table. She would have turned into Suzanne and Blaine and Mandy—Girls Who Liked Boys. Dinah was the Girl Who Didn't Like Boys. The Girl Who Didn't Go to Dances with Boys. She imagined herself walking into the sock hop alone, head held high, and having all the giggling couples there fall silent as she entered the gym all by herself, proud in her famous spinsterhood.

Maybe there would be a biography of Dinah someday: *Dinah Seabrooke, Spinster Girl*. She'd be like Queen Elizabeth the First, who never married and, if Dinah remembered rightly, cut off the heads of any men who wanted to marry her.

And suddenly, for no reason at all, Dinah burst into tears.

But Dynamite Dinah was hardly the type for crying. Friday morning she hopped out of bed early, ready to pour all her energy into preparing for the capital punishment debate and rehearsing for the play. During

English class she furtively scribbled notes on index cards about the need for the death penalty; during gym class she recited Wilfredo Desperado's lines out in center field. At night she slept with two books under her pillow: her script for *Love Saves the Day* and her precious library book, *Capital Punishment: For and Against*.

Dinah started reading the book in earnest over the weekend. It was a hard book, written for grown-ups and not for middle-school students. But she looked up the big words in the dictionary, words like *unconstitutional* and *deterrent* and *retribution*. Dinah liked big words. She had memorized the Gettysburg Address once just for the sound of the strange and mysterious words in it: "We cannot *dedicate*, we cannot *consecrate*, we cannot *hallow* this ground." The words in the capital punishment book were just as grand. Dinah felt they gave her a secret power over Nick, a magical weapon to win the debate.

First Dinah read all the articles in the "For" part of the book. When she'd finished she was even more in favor of capital punishment than she had been before. She wanted to *do* something about capital punishment, to make sure it stayed legal. For starters, at least, she could write to her congressperson.

During the winter Mr. Dixon had had all the students in the class write to their congressperson on some important issue of their own choosing. Dinah had written her letter on recycling, and Representative Myers had written back, too—a nice letter saying that he agreed with Dinah completely. Dinah found the letter in her desk Saturday afternoon and took it down-stairs to the computer. Representative Myers was about to get another letter, this time on capital punishment:

Dear Rep. Myers:

Thank you for your letter about recycling. Today I have something else important to write to you about. I am strongly in favor of capital punishment, and I hope you are, too.

The murder rate in this country keeps going up. The death penalty rate keeps going down. Don't you think that means we need more capital punishment, not less? The best way to stop crime is to punish criminals.

I am resolved that capital punishment should *not* be abolished. In seven years I will vote for you if you agree.

Sincerely,
Dinah Seabrooke

As soon as the letter was printed and in its envelope, Dinah took Benjamin with her to mail it. She lifted him up high so he could help drop it into the corner mailbox. There! Representative Myers was sure to be convinced. All Dinah had to do now was convince Mr. Dixon and the rest of the sixth-period social studies class, if they even needed to be convinced. How could anybody *not* be in favor of capital punishment? Nick might as well give up right now and surrender unconditionally.

Dinah was curious, though, about what the "Against" part of the book had to say. As far as she was concerned, they could have just skipped the "Against" part altogether. But the articles opposing capital punishment took up the whole second half of the book.

Dinah read them on Sunday, during the quiet lull of Benjamin's nap. When she did, she was amazed. The "Against" articles said that in reality the death penalty didn't stop murderers from murdering. Either criminals didn't think ahead of time about the punishment they were going to get, because they were so filled with hate and rage, or because they didn't expect to be caught, or else they thought life imprisonment was just as bad as being executed. Murder rates had gone up in the past twenty years, but so had the rates of all other crimes, crimes like burglary and mugging, which had never been punished by the death penalty in the first place. The book said there was no difference in murder rates, none at all, between states that had capital punishment and states that didn't. That seemed impossible to Dinah. But the book said it was true.

Dinah took the book downstairs to show her father, who was changing Benjamin's diaper after his nap.

"That doesn't make sense," her father agreed. "If the death penalty doesn't make any difference, it's only because hardly anybody ever gets it. Those guys expect to get off with a slap on the wrist because usually they do. If they knew they were definitely going straight to the electric chair, we'd see a big difference in crime rates, believe you me."

Dinah believed him. If William MacGregor ever put together a sequel to *Capital Punishment: For and Against*, she and her father could coauthor an article for it. Maybe the sequel could be called *Capital Punishment: For, For, For!*

During one study period in the school library early the next week, Dinah saw Nick copying entries on capital punishment out of the *Reader's Guide to Periodical Literature.* She smiled to herself.

"Hey, Ocean-River," Nick asked when he saw her watching him. "About the debate. Are you finding any good stuff?"

"Maybe I am and maybe I'm not," Dinah said mysteriously.

"I found a couple of articles, but they aren't very good. The public library has a book on capital punishment that sounded really terrific, but somebody else already has it checked out."

Dinah tried not to let her face show any glee.

"It's you. You checked it out."

"Maybe I did and maybe I didn't."

She wondered if Nick would ask her if he could borrow the book for a couple of days, but he didn't.

"Okay, Ocean-River," he said. "It's only fair that you get some extra help. I was in a debate last fall at my old school, and let me tell you, there was nothing left of my opponent when I was done. Not even a small, sticky puddle on the floor."

"Is that so?"

"I cannot tell a lie. Besides, I got the easy side on this one."

Dinah was astonished. "You really think so? You're *against* capital punishment?"

Now it was Nick's turn to look surprised. "Aren't

97

you? I mean, murder is murder. Somebody murders somebody, and then the government says to the murderer, 'Murder is wrong!' and then to show how wrong it is, they turn around and murder the murderer. It's stupid. All they've done is turn into murderers themselves."

"But the first murderer was guilty. He *deserves* to die."

"Just because a court says he's guilty doesn't mean he really is. Juries can make mistakes."

Nick had a point there.

"But most times, you know," Dinah said. "You know the guy is guilty. Somebody saw him do it, or he confessed, or something."

"Yeah," Nick said. "But you still don't really know why he did it. For all you know, you might have done the same thing if you were him. The only good thing I can think of about capital punishment is I guess it lowers the crime rate. But, like, by how much? What does your book say?"

"I haven't read that part of it yet," Dinah lied. It was too much to expect her to hand Nick the best argument against capital punishment on a silver platter.

"You're tough, Ocean-River," Nick said then, pulling out another volume of the *Reader's Guide*. "I'd better not murder anyone around you. You'd be all set to strap me into the electric chair and push the button. But after the debate, we'll see who's tough. We'll see who believes in capital punishment then."

But Dinah thought that Nick looked worried.

11

The play was to be performed Friday, in a special assembly during eighth period. The cast and crew rehearsed furiously to be ready in time. And throughout, no crew member was more polite or cooperative than Nick Tribble. The props Nick was responsible for were always in place; the set changes he helped with were carried out perfectly. All week long there wasn't a single joke, or smart-aleck remark, or teasing comment, or burp.

"You've reformed," Dinah said to him, partway through one rehearsal.

"So would a lot of criminals if you gave them the chance," Nick said. "But you can't reform someone after he's dead."

The dress rehearsal after school on Thursday, their only rehearsal in full costume, was a nightmarish disaster. Todd made two late entrances. Paul forgot half his lines. Suzanne tore her dress on a nail. The set of Olivia's farmhouse almost fell over during the closing scene.

"I ask only . . . your love," Manly declared.

"Wait!" Olivia shrieked. "The house is tipping over!"

Though the set only wobbled and didn't actually come crashing to the floor, the near-catastrophe certainly spoiled the mood of the lovers' kiss.

"Wonderful!" Mrs. Bevens said after the practice curtain call at the end. "The old saying goes, 'The worse the dress rehearsal, the better the show!'"

Dinah and Suzanne were unconvinced.

"She just said that to make us feel better," Dinah told Suzanne on the bus ride home. "But I don't feel better. Do you?"

Suzanne shook her head. "If we live through this, I'm going to stick with my piano lessons. At least the piano doesn't start to fall on you during a recital. And you don't have to kiss the piano in front of two hundred fifty people. What if everyone laughs when Todd and I kiss tomorrow?"

"It's supposed to be a funny play," Dinah said. "I think it would be worse if they didn't laugh."

"So what if they *don't* laugh?"

"They will," Dinah said. But she didn't want them to laugh just because Paul forgot his lines and the set wobbled. She wanted them to laugh because Dinah Seabrooke was an actress of rare and wonderful comic gifts.

The cast and crew were excused from afternoon classes on Friday. Somehow Dinah survived her morning classes, though Mr. Prensky had to call her to attention twice during first-period English. At lunch, Dinah, Suzanne, and Mandy barely touched their food.

"You're going to be great," Blaine told them as they took their trays to the conveyor belt. "All of you."

"You're not supposed to say that," Dinah corrected her. "You're supposed to say, 'Break a leg.'"

"Why would you want someone to break a leg?" Blaine asked, obviously confused.

"Just say it," Dinah said. "It's for good luck."

"Break a leg, then," Blaine said.

Backstage, Mrs. Bevens adjusted their costumes and applied makeup.

"Suzanne, make sure they can hear you in the back of the auditorium. Paul, if you forget a line, don't panic. Just listen for my prompting, say it, and go on. Dinah, remember not to talk too fast. You're going to do a splendid job today, all of you."

"What if the set falls over?" Mandy asked.

"It won't," Mrs. Bevens promised. "And if it does, just pretend you don't notice it and keep on. At all costs, keep on."

"Even if we're crushed underneath it, dead?" Paul asked.

Mrs. Bevens didn't hear him. "Places," she said. "We're about to begin."

And as Mrs. Bevens had predicted, the play was as wonderful as the dress rehearsal had been terrible. Todd entered on time. Suzanne's dress didn't tear. Paul forgot some of his lines, but the audience was laughing so hard at all the rest that nobody realized or cared.

They laughed hardest of all for Dinah. From the moment of his first mustache-twirling entrance, the play belonged to Wilfredo Desperado. All Dinah had to do was stroke her mustache or waggle her matching bushy black fake eyebrows, and the entire sixth grade rocked with laughter. When Wilfredo threatened Olivia with foreclosure on her mortgage, they hissed. When Wilfredo tied Olivia to a tree, they booed. When at last he was vanquished utterly and stomped about the stage in a rage of humiliated defeat, they stamped their feet and whistled.

The louder the audience stamped, the louder Dinah stomped. Perhaps she stomped too hard. Suddenly the farmhouse began to fall, so quickly that she couldn't remember afterward exactly what had happened. All she knew was that Nick sprang forward from the wings swiftly enough to catch it before it struck her.

The narrowness of Dinah's escape stunned her. For a moment she forgot she was Wilfredo. She was only a girl who might have been injured if it hadn't been for the quick action of—this boy, who now stood a few inches from her, supporting the weight of the set with his two hands, smiling down at her smugly.

Dinah couldn't remember her next line. All she could think of was: "You saved . . . my life. How can I ever thank you?"

And then Nick would take her in his arms, except that he already had the set in his arms. And he wasn't Manly, and she wasn't Olivia; he was obnoxious Nick Tribble, and she was Dinah Seabrooke, who was wearing a mustache and who didn't like boys, anyway.

From the wings, Dinah heard Mrs. Bevens prompting her: "Oh, cursed be they who have foiled the plot of Wilfredo Desperado!"

Dinah repeated the line mechanically and made her exit. The audience clapped for her, as the rest of the crew helped Nick right the set. Backstage, Mrs. Bevens gave Dinah a reassuring hug, and Suzanne squeezed her hand.

The play drew to its close. The kiss between Manly and Olivia might have been the first kiss in the history of the world. "Oooooh!" The gasps and squeals that ran through the auditorium were so satisfying that quiet, serious Todd turned to the crowd, grinned, and kissed Suzanne again.

For the curtain call, each actor came forward still in character—first Heather, who played the fortune-teller, then Mandy as the mother, Paul as Humphrey, then Manly and Olivia holding hands, and finally, last of all, Wilfredo himself, still twirling his mustache, his eyes still gleaming with memories of evil deeds gone by and dreams of evil deeds to come.

The exuberant applause gave way to cheers, and more cheers. Compared to this, what was any sock hop? Compared to this, what was any boy?

Dinah kept her mustache on at the cast party afterward. She might never take it off. It was odd to think that just a week ago she had cared about being pretty. Let other girls be pretty, girls who weren't lucky enough to have stolen the show and brought down the house in a Tony Award–worthy performance.

Nick came up behind Dinah at the party.

"Boo!" he said.

Dinah jumped. Then she blushed. She knew she had to thank Nick for catching the falling set in time, but she didn't know what to say. She didn't want to make a big mushy *thing* out of it.

"Boo yourself," she finally said. "I mean, thank you. You know, for before. When the set was falling on me."

"No problem, Ocean-River," Nick said. "Any time a set starts to fall on you, just holler, and I'll be there." Then, as if he was afraid of sounding too mushy himself, Nick said, "Oh, by the way, Ocean-River, if Manly hadn't saved Olivia from the forest fire, your Wilfredo would have faced a pretty bad murder rap. He was the one who tied her to the tree and set the fire."

"So?" Dinah asked.

"So according to people like you, Wilfredo Desperado should get capital punishment."

Then Nick was off to the refreshment table to grab another few handfuls of cookies and guzzle down another few cups of fruit punch.

Dinah's parents had both come to the play, with Mrs. Briscoe.

Mrs. Briscoe took Dinah's hands in hers. "Bravo, Dinah!"

"Benjamin missed quite a performance," Dinah's mother said, hugging her. "But we'll show him the videotape."

Her father kissed her. "You're something else," he told her. "Watch out, world!"

Dinah's sentiments, exactly.

Suzanne's parents hugged her, too. Todd introduced her to his father: "Dad, this is the girl I told you about." Mandy's father said Dinah should go to

Broadway. Paul's mother said Dinah should go to Hollywood.

Yes, sock hop or no sock hop, things were turning out quite nicely.

12

"Nick rescued you," Suzanne said solemnly as they walked to the parking lot after the cast party.

"It could have been anybody," Dinah said. "I mean, anybody standing that close to the stage would have helped anybody about to have a house fall on them. It didn't have to be Nick and me."

"But it was," Suzanne said.

"That was your Nick?" Dinah's mother asked, falling into step with the girls. "That nice boy who was so quick on his feet?"

"He's not *my* Nick," Dinah said. "Anyway, you don't have to like someone just because he rescues you."

Suzanne thought for a minute. "In books, you do. I think in books the girl almost always marries the boy who rescues her. Maybe not in the first book, but in the sequel."

"Really, girls," Dinah's mother said. "This sounds awfully sexist to me. Girls can rescue boys, too, you know. As far as that goes, boys can rescue boys and girls can rescue girls. There doesn't have to be any fixed gender role in rescuing."

"I've read a couple of books where the princess rescues the prince," Suzanne offered.

"See?" Dinah's mother said.

"They weren't very good," Suzanne said.

"In stories where the princess rescues the prince, do they get married at the end?" Dinah asked.

"Not always. But usually."

"Oh, girls," Dinah's mother said, as they reached the cars. "Most of the time in life, people rescue themselves. You can't expect to be Sleeping Beauty or Cinderella waiting for a prince to come along and change your life."

"We know," Dinah and Suzanne said together.

"But Dinah didn't rescue herself from that falling set today," Suzanne added, opening her car door. "Nick rescued her."

And in the maddening way she had of getting the last word in an argument, Suzanne shut the door and her parents drove away.

There was only one thing to be done. Some way, somehow, Dinah had to rescue Nick. Dinah didn't know if there were any books with double rescues in them, where the boy rescued the girl and then the girl rescued the boy, but it seemed to her that the second rescue would cancel out the first. Two rescues would be the same as no rescue, and nobody would have to marry anybody.

What could Dinah rescue Nick from? It was too much to hope that a set would fall on Nick just as Dinah was walking by. Maybe a *tree* would fall on Nick and Dinah could leap forward to save him? No. Dinah might as well hope for a falling meteorite.

Or . . . what if Dinah *caused* a set or tree or meteorite to fall on Nick, and then, lo and behold, there she would be, right on the spot to save him. Not a meteorite, of course, but *something*. For example, a pail of water set over a doorway. Or some other clever, cunning booby trap. Dinah would set the trap and let Nick happen along. Then, just as he was about to be caught in it, Dinah would save him.

But Dinah knew in advance that a booby trap wouldn't work. With her luck, she'd get caught in her own trap just as Nick was happening along, and he'd end up rescuing her a second time. Dinah could imagine what Suzanne would have to say about that. Anyway, Dinah had to spend the coming week in final preparations for the capital punishment debate. She couldn't spend it figuring out how to make a foolproof booby trap.

It was going to be an exciting week for Dinah. Thursday was the capital punishment debate with Nick, and Friday night was the dance. *And* at last, at last, this of all weeks was the week for Dinah to read morning announcements. A debate, a dance, and morning announcements all in the same week. This was Dinah's idea of what a week should be, perhaps minus the dance.

When Dinah arrived at school Monday morning, she headed straight to the office to prepare for morning announcements. Mr. Roemer, the principal, winked at her as she passed his office on her way to the small room where the announcements were broadcast. School principals always knew who Dinah was.

Mrs. Bevens greeted Dinah and showed her how the microphone worked. When it was turned on, everything Dinah said would be piped into every single room in JFK Middle School. Mrs. Bevens handed Dinah the typed list of the day's announcements. At the top of the page Dinah read to herself: "Please rise and salute the flag. I pledge allegiance to the flag of the United States of America, and to the republic for which it stands, one nation, under God, indivisible, with liberty and justice for all."

Dinah looked up from her text. "Doesn't everybody already know the words to the Pledge of Allegiance? You say it fifty million times in elementary school."

Mrs. Bevens shook her head. "You'd be surprised how easy it is to forget your own name and phone number when the mike is turned on and you're performing live."

Dinah Seabrooke, performing live. Dinah felt a pleasurable shiver of anticipation.

"Now, Dinah, dear, try to read nice and slowly," Mrs. Bevens said. "Read about twice as slowly as you feel you should, and you'll probably get it just right."

Dinah was famous for her fast talking. In elementary school she had set records with her high-speed recitation of the Gettysburg Address.

Dinah practiced with the pledge. "I . . . pledge . . . allegiance . . . to . . . the . . . flag," she read, with a long pause after each word.

"Perfect," Mrs. Bevens said.

The enormous clock on the wall said five to eight.

"Five more minutes," Dinah said. The minute hand lurched ahead one line. "Four."

At eight o'clock, the bell rang.

"Wait for the second bell," Mrs. Bevens said.

Dinah read the list of announcements over and over again to herself. Softball; Chess Club; track and field; Environmental Action Club; a pitch for Friday's dance written by its publicity chairperson, Dinah Seabrooke herself. Dinah had to admit the dance announcement was nothing special. It wasn't musical; it didn't rhyme; it wasn't funny. But over the weekend Dinah had worked too much on the debate to have any energy left over for anything else. Some days there was a disciplinary announcement made by Mr. Roemer, explaining one of the school rules or chastising students for bad behavior. Today the announcements belonged to Dinah alone.

Morning announcements were always so dull. Was this Dinah's chance to add some spice and sparkle to the same old routine reading of the day's ho-hum news? Maybe she should use her Wilfredo Desperado voice. It would be funny to hear Wilfredo leading the school in the Pledge of Allegiance. It seemed too boring and un-Dinah-like, after everything else that had happened in sixth grade, just to get up and read the typewritten list of announcements in her own ordinary voice. On the other hand, if she tried anything too alarming, Mrs. Bevens and Mr. Roemer might decide that one day of Dinah's morning announcements was all that JFK Middle School could stand. Dinah had all week to think of her own special touch for morning announcements. For now, it would be enough to read the Pledge of Allegiance nice and slowly.

The second bell rang. Mrs. Bevens turned on the mike and slipped away to her chair on the other side of the room. Dinah looked over at her, fighting a sudden surge of panic. Mrs. Bevens gave her an encouraging nod.

"Please . . . rise . . . and . . . salute . . . the . . . flag."

Dinah's voice came out in a hoarse croak but grew in steadiness as she read the familiar words of the pledge. Mrs. Bevens had been right. If the words hadn't been written down right in front of her, Dinah would have forgotten them. Their very familiarity almost made them easier to forget. After so many recitations they had become sounds, not words, just a collection of meaningless syllables.

"Please . . . be . . . seated."

Dinah waited to let the seven hundred fifty students of JFK Middle School obey her command. She thought of the school's long, mazelike hallways in which she had been so lost as a new student last fall. Now in every single homeroom, sixth, seventh, and even eighth graders were listening to her voice—Dinah's voice—reading the announcements of the day.

"The girls' softball team will play Hillside this afternoon at four o'clock, away."

Mrs. Bevens mouthed the words *Slow down* at her.

"Today's . . . meeting . . . of . . . the . . . Chess . . . Club . . . is . . . canceled."

Mrs. Bevens signaled with her circled thumb and forefinger: Okay.

Dinah got through the rest of the announcements without incident. "This is Dinah Seabrooke," she read from the printed sheet, in conclusion. "Have a good day."

Mrs. Bevens turned off the mike for her. "Very nice, Dinah, dear. Very businesslike and professional."

Dinah accepted the compliment with a modest smile. "Businesslike and professional" was all well and good. But she herself expected more from Dynamite Dinah.

13

Mr. Dixon was out that Monday. The substitute gave the class one last study period to prepare for the debates. Dinah used the time to memorize her prepared opening statement. Nick, she saw, was still working furiously on his, scribbling out whole paragraphs and tearing marked-up pages in half. He folded one crumpled page into a paper airplane and sent it soaring toward the recycling bin; apparently the substitute didn't know Mr. Dixon's views on paper airplanes.

It was obvious that Nick was still far from ready for Thursday's match.

The debates began the next day, on Tuesday, with Blaine and Artie facing off on the topic of gun control, Artie arguing in favor of gun control and Blaine against. Dinah's parents believed in gun control, and Dinah did, too. As far as Dinah was concerned, there were no good arguments on the other side. Dinah knew that Blaine personally felt the same way. But Mr. Dixon had assigned Blaine the anti-gun-control position, so for the length of the debate Blaine was as convincing an opponent of gun control as Dinah had ever seen.

"Guns don't kill people. People kill people," Blaine said. Dinah had heard that line before, but when Blaine said it, it sounded sensible and true. That was the thing about Blaine: Everything she said sounded sensible and true. Sometimes Dinah wished she could be like Blaine. Everyone respected Blaine, which was why they had elected her class president last fall. Boys didn't tease Blaine the way they did Dinah. They didn't call her Blaine-the-Pain or throw things at her head. When Blaine asked a boy to a dance, the boy said yes, and that was the end of it.

When the debate was done, Mr. Dixon asked the class to vote for the winner.

"Sorry, Adams," he told Artie with a grin, once he had counted all the ballots. "It's twenty-six to two in favor of Yarborough. And with my vote, twenty-seven."

By Wednesday, Dinah was used to reading morning announcements. She felt as if she had been reading morning announcements all her life. Mrs. Bevens only had to signal twice for Dinah to slow down, and Dinah's friends no longer stopped her in the hall to exclaim how strange and funny it was to hear her voice come booming over the PA system.

Wednesday's debate was between Jason Winfield and Katie Richards, on the legalization of drugs.

"Oh, Nick," Dinah heard Katie telling Nick before the bell, "I'm really scared."

"You'll do fine," Nick told her. "Dixon's bark is worse than his bite. He shouts a lot, but he grades pretty easy. Besides, Jason's nothing that great."

"And I have a sore throat, too," Katie went on. "I hope it's better by the dance on Friday. Feel my hand. It's burning."

Dinah didn't turn around to see if Nick touched Katie's hand or not.

"Look at it this way," Nick said. "Either way it will be over in forty minutes."

The bell rang. Mr. Dixon rapped on his desk. Dinah waited for the debate to begin. She hoped both Jason *and* Katie would lose. Could both sides lose in a debate? Dinah still hadn't forgiven Jason for turning down her invitation to the dance, and while Katie was perfectly free to invite any boy she wanted—and Dinah herself had had no intention of inviting Nick—still, something about Katie got on Dinah's nerves. She didn't like Katie's heart-shaped earrings. She didn't like the pink laces in Katie's shoes.

Mr. Dixon took a seat in the rear of the room. "Resolved: The use of marijuana, cocaine, and heroin should be legalized. All right, Winfield, Richards. Enlighten us, please."

Dinah couldn't see that much enlightenment came from either Jason or Katie. Katie kept saying over and over again that drugs were just immoral and no one should use them and *she* would certainly never use them. Jason kept saying that marijuana wasn't any worse than alcohol, and alcohol was legal, so marijuana should be legal, too. Dinah tried to watch Mr. Dixon's face to see what he was thinking. But he didn't scowl any more than he usually did.

When it was time for the vote, Dinah grudgingly cast hers for Jason. He hadn't done a good job, but he had done a better job than Katie.

"Winfield, eighteen; Richards, ten. And my vote? Winfield. But the Lincoln-Douglas debates, this wasn't. Okay, kids, tomorrow: Tribble and Seabrooke."

That night in her room after dinner, Dinah looked through the neat stack of index cards she had made from *Capital Punishment: For and Against*. She would sleep with the book under her pillow one last time, for good measure. Maybe at that moment Nick was reading and rereading the couple of crummy articles he had found in the *Reader's Guide*. It wouldn't do him much good to sleep with them under his pillow.

Nick Tribble, prepare to meet thy doom! Dinah gave her best Wilfredo Desperado cackle.

And yet, it would be more fun to trounce Nick in a more equal contest. It would hardly count as winning to beat someone who hadn't even had a chance to prepare for the fight. Dinah had always thought of herself as a fair person, and it didn't feel fair to have such an overwhelming advantage over Nick. Maybe Dinah should have shared the book with Nick, after all, weeks ago, when she had first stumbled upon it in the library. If Suzanne had been in Dinah's place, Suzanne would have shared the book with her opponent—even if the opponent was Nick. But it was too late now.

Or was it? Dinah could still share the book with Nick, at least for one night. Dinah knew from her classes with him that Nick was smart and quick. Even one evening with *Capital Punishment: For and Against* would make a big difference. It would rescue Nick from certain disaster during sixth period tomorrow.

It would *rescue* Nick from certain disaster. Why hadn't Dinah thought of it before? Sharing the book with Nick would be rescuing him in turn. It wasn't as dramatic as cutting the ropes that bound someone to a tree with a forest fire approaching. Or leaping forward to catch a falling farmhouse as it was about to crush someone. But, technically, it would count as a rescue. Dinah would be the princess rescuing the prince. At least, she'd be the princess rescuing the frog.

"I have to go drop something off on Barclay Court," Dinah told her parents as they sat together in the family room watching the news on TV in peace and quiet, now that Benjamin was in bed. "I'll be back in ten minutes."

"Who do you know on Barclay Court?" her mother asked.

"Just someone in one of my classes at school. Bye!"

It was a golden spring evening. The dogwood trees were in bloom—some with pale pink blossoms, some with white—and so were the azaleas. Running, Dinah passed some boys playing catch in a dead-end street and a high-school couple holding hands. She had to run: The fire was raging closer; the capital punishment debate was less than twenty-four hours away.

Dinah had looked up Nick's address in the phone

book before she left. His house, at 26 Barclay Court, turned out to be a pleasant, two-story brick home, with a basketball hoop hung over the two-car garage. But Nick wasn't outside shooting baskets. He was inside, Dinah knew, frantically, desperately, hopelessly preparing for the debate.

Nick Tribble, rescue is on the way!

Dinah stood for a long moment on Nick's front steps. Should she leave the book on the steps and then ring the bell and run away? She wouldn't be able to run fast and far enough to escape without being seen. Maybe she'd leave the book, ring the bell, and then hide in the bushes. Hiding in bushes was a tradition now for her and Nick.

Dinah lay the book smack in the middle of the welcome mat. Quickly, she rang the bell and darted behind the larger of the two pink azalea bushes flanking the front door. She crouched down behind it and waited.

Nick's father opened the door. At first he didn't see the book. He looked down the front walk to the street, shook his head, and turned away. But as he turned, the book caught his eye. He picked it up, puzzled; then, reading the title, he grinned.

"Nick!" he called from the doorway. "Someone left you a book."

"What?" Dinah heard Nick holler.

In a minute Nick was there at the door, taking the book from his father.

"Did you see her?" Nick asked. "Did you see the girl who left it?"

"Nope. When I opened the door, there was no one in sight."

Nick's father went back inside, but Nick stayed behind on the front steps.

"Hey, Dad!" he called after his father. "Do you mind if I water the big azalea bush? It's looking very dry."

Then, more softly, "Thanks, Ocean-River. See you at school tomorrow."

Nick disappeared inside. Dinah waited until the coast seemed clear, then she slipped out from behind the azalea bush and hurried back home.

Rescue of frog by princess completed.

14

That night Dinah couldn't tuck *Capital Punishment: For and Against* under her pillow before she went to bed. So she contented herself with sleeping on her stack of index cards instead. All night long she dreamed about the debate. In the dream she'd start out as Dinah debating Nick, but then Nick would turn into Mr. Briscoe waving an ear of red corn as he debated, and Dinah would turn into Wilfredo Desperado, and Nick would turn into Manly, and Dinah would turn into Olivia—all talking heatedly about capital punishment as Mr. Dixon looked on, score sheet in hand.

"Who won?" Dinah's father asked at breakfast, after she had told him about her dream.

"I woke up before I found out," Dinah said.

"In a way, it doesn't matter who wins," Dinah's mother said. "This is part of your work in social studies, so what matters is what you learn about capital punishment and about debating, win *or* lose."

Dinah stared at her mother in disbelief. She had never heard anything more ridiculous. Winning the debate with Nick was *everything*. But her mother had only meant to be helpful, so Dinah kindly ignored her and ran outside for the bus.

"I wish I were in your social studies class," Suzanne said as the bus neared school. "I wish I could see the debate."

"I wish you could, too," Dinah said. "I wish Mr. Dixon were having it videotaped."

Dinah half felt like announcing her debate with Nick as the headline event of the day at JFK Middle School, but decided against it. It might give Nick the wrong idea; it might make him think he was more important in Dinah's life than he really was. Besides, Dinah still had one more day of morning announcements to savor. Had any morning announcers ever been fired from the job before their week was through? Dinah didn't want to be the first.

In first-period English Nick looked tired, but confident.

"Here's your book." He gave it to Dinah. "I stayed up until two o'clock this morning, and believe me, I have it memorized."

"What year was the Supreme Court decision upholding the constitutionality of capital punishment?" Dinah asked him as a test.

"Nineteen seventy-three," Nick shot back.

Maybe he did have it memorized.

At lunch Dinah tuned out the others' conversations and recited her opening speech over and over again in her head.

"I wish I could sound like you," Dinah told Blaine suddenly.

"Like me?" Blaine sounded genuinely surprised. "I wish I could sound like you."

"Everything you say always sounds like it's true," Dinah said. "You always sound so smart, and everyone listens when you talk and takes you seriously."

"If they can stay awake," Blaine said. "You're the one who's always funny and interesting."

Dinah couldn't contradict Blaine on that. But capital punishment wasn't a funny topic. The debate wouldn't be won or lost by a tally of who made the wittiest opening speech or the most jokes in the rebuttal period.

"Oh, by the way, Dinah," Blaine said then. "Guess who has strep throat and can't go to the sock hop?"

"Amory Cruz?"

"Katie Richards."

"Katie?"

"She called me last night. Her sore throat turned out to be strep, and her mother said she can't go."

"That's too bad," Dinah said automatically. As a matter of fact, she wouldn't mind coming down with strep herself—or scarlet fever?—sometime between morning announcements tomorrow morning and the dance tomorrow night. It seemed like one of the more convenient ways to get out of going to the dance. Maybe Dinah could bring her morning announcements to an unforgettable close by collapsing right on the air.

"So you could still ask Nick if you wanted to," Suzanne reminded Dinah. "He's going alone now, too."

Dinah felt like sticking her fingers into her ears to shut out Suzanne's suggestion.

"I already had my chance to ask Nick. I went to a lot of trouble *not* to ask Nick. You think I'm going to ask him the day before the dance?"

"Why not?" Suzanne said.

"Besides, Katie can't help having strep. Nick's *her* boyfriend. It wouldn't be fair to ask him." Dinah was glad to have another argument at hand.

"I wouldn't say he's her *boy*friend," Blaine said. "Actually, I don't think she even likes Nick all that much anymore. She likes Jason now, after the debate and all."

"But he beat her in the debate," Dinah said.

"She said she thinks she fell in love with him between the first and second rebuttal. So watch out, Dinah. You never know what can happen in a debate."

"Did you fall in love with Artie in your debate?" Dinah asked.

"No," answered Blaine. "But it would be pretty hard for anyone to fall in love with Artie."

Dinah stood up to carry her tray to the conveyor belt. It *would* be pretty hard for anyone to fall in love with Artie. And it would be pretty hard for Dinah to fall in love with anyone.

By now the class was used to the routine for the debates. Mr. Dixon set two chairs in the front of the room, one on either side of his desk. On his desk he placed a podium, where the two debaters would take turns speaking. Then he took a seat at an empty desk in the back of the room.

"Resolved," his voice boomed out majestically, "capital punishment should be abolished. Affirmative, Nick Tribble. Negative, Dinah Seabrooke. Tribble, Seabrooke: Take it away."

Nick stood up and walked to the podium. Without looking at Dinah, he began to read his opening speech. He read it with no show of emotion, as if he were merely pointing out obvious truths that everybody in the world but Dinah knew all along. But Dinah saw that Nick's hands were shaking as he turned the pages of his speech, even though his voice was steady.

"Capital punishment should be abolished. First of all, it doesn't work. It doesn't deter crime. Second of all, courts can make mistakes, and if you execute an innocent person, you can never bring that person back and make it right again. Third, it says in the Bible 'Thou shalt not kill.' It doesn't say, 'Thou shalt not kill except in the case of capital punishment.'"

Nick went through each of his three points in turn. He quoted all the facts about crime rates from the "Against" section of *Capital Punishment: For and Against*. They had struck Dinah powerfully the first time she read them; listening to Nick now, Dinah was hit hard by them for a second time. It definitely seemed that, as far as crime prevention went, capital punishment was a failure. Had she made a mistake in sharing the book with Nick? It might have cost her the debate. But in an odd way Dinah felt proud of Nick's speech, and proud that she deserved a small part of the credit for it.

Nick talked about the danger of executing an innocent person. Dinah thought his arguments there were pretty weak. One time in a thousand, you might execute an innocent person. But the other 999 times you were executing someone guilty.

And yet, even a guilty person was a *person*. Wilfredo Desperado was a person. Well, not a real person, just a made-up person; but if he had been real, he would have been a person. He would have had thoughts and feelings and hopes and fears. It would be a terrible thing to know that at a certain moment on a certain day, you were going to stop being a person, to know for a fact that you had only a month or a day or an hour more to live.

Nick talked about the electric chair. There had been a few graphic descriptions of what it was like to die in the electric chair in *Capital Punishment: For and Against*, but Dinah had skipped over them. She didn't like to read gross and horrible things. But as Nick gave his painful examples, Dinah couldn't skip a single detail. The electric chair sounded monstrously cruel and barbaric. Dinah wouldn't have wanted Wilfredo Desperado to die in the electric chair. When it came right down to it, she didn't want anyone to die that way.

Had she really thought that Nick Tribble didn't have feelings? No one could describe a death row prisoner's feelings the way Nick did unless he knew a lot about feelings himself.

Nick came to the last line of his speech: "Capital punishment is just a fancy word for *murder*."

Then he sat down, without smiling.

Dinah stood up at the podium, her speech in front of her, with Nick just a few feet away, sitting in readiness for his turn at rebuttal. Her speech was good. It might even be as good as Nick's had been. But Dinah wasn't sure she wanted to give it. She wasn't sure she believed in capital punishment anymore. Maybe capital punishment *was* a fancy word for murder. Maybe every person, even a bad and evil person, had a right to life that no one else should ever take away.

"Seabrooke?" Mr. Dixon said.

Dinah began to read.

She quoted the Bible, too: "'An eye for an eye, a tooth for a tooth.' And I would say: a life for a life. Someone who commits a crime deserves to be punished in kind. Someone who takes another person's life deserves to give up his own life. A murderer deserves to *die*."

She felt herself speeding up as she went along. She felt herself sounding emotional like Dinah, not calm and controlled like Blaine. But her emotion was a kind of playacting. It was as if she were following stage directions written into her speech: Read with emotion. It was the emotion she would have had if she had still believed in capital punishment.

Dinah talked about the cost of keeping a criminal in prison for life and about the likelihood of early parole even in a life sentence. She gave examples of released

126

killers who had gone on to kill again and of the anguish of their victims' families. Her stories were as gripping as Nick's stories had been. But in a way, they were beside the point. Yes, the murderers' victims had suffered. But capital punishment wasn't going to bring the dead back from their graves. No second murder could make the first murder go away.

"Opponents of capital punishment would have us pity the murderer. How about pitying his victims instead?"

Then Dinah sat down, trembling.

Next came the rebuttals. This was the hard part. Now, speaking only from their hastily scribbled notes, Nick and Dinah each had to take the other's points one by one and demolish them. That was hard enough. Harder still was demolishing the other person's arguments when you were starting to believe them.

Nick went first. "My *opponent* claims that it's expensive to keep a person alive in prison. We're supposed to *kill* someone just to save *money?*" Nick sounded so scornful that for a moment Dinah felt a last flicker of hatred toward him, as if she were back at her father's store with an exercise bra dangling from her head. And then, just like that, the hatred extinguished itself. Nick's scorn was a kind of playacting, too. Dinah knew that he knew that she had given a good speech. What he didn't know was that she no longer believed a word of it.

When Dinah's turn came to rebut Nick's argument, she sounded just as scornful. "My *opponent* claims that we should abolish capital punishment because we might make a mistake and execute the wrong person. Has this ever happened? Can he point to one single solitary case where this actually happened?"

Back and forth they went. Dinah felt as if every cell in her body were fully and triumphantly alive and singing. Debating was like acting in a play, but even more exhilarating. In a play Dinah recited lines someone else had written. Here she was making up her own script as she went along, just as Nick was making up his script. It was as if she and Nick were the two stars of the play, making up its script together.

Dinah wished that she and Nick were going to debate every topic Mr. Dixon had assigned: gun control, drugs, welfare, animal rights. Even capital punishment over and over again. Maybe some talent scout was listening outside the school windows, ready to fly them to Hollywood for a major motion picture: *Debate: The Movie.*

And then it was over, and Dinah and Nick sank into their seats.

"All right, class," Mr. Dixon barked. "Mark your ballots and pass them back to me."

Dinah waited as Mr. Dixon counted the votes. But her mother had been right. It didn't really matter how the others voted, or what Mr. Dixon decided. In a way, Dinah had to admit that she had lost the debate: Nick had convinced her that capital punishment should be abolished. If that wasn't winning a debate, what was? But Dinah knew she had done a good job. She had done her best, and Dynamite Dinah's best was pretty spectacular. Even if now she was going to have to write another letter to Representative Myers, promising to vote for him in seven years if he did the opposite of everything she had told him to do in her last letter.

Mr. Dixon cleared his throat.

"Seabrooke, fifteen. Tribble, thirteen."

So Dinah had won the class vote. But it was close, as close as it could be without being a tie.

"And the real winner is . . . " Dixon paused. "Frankly, I'd have to give it a draw. Class, what you have just heard was a *debate*. Thank you, Nick and Dinah."

It was the only time all year, as far as Dinah could remember, that Mr. Dixon had ever used first names.

The bell rang.

Nick held out his hand to Dinah. "Congratulations, Ocean-River," he said. "You did great."

Dinah was holding her books in her right hand, so she offered Nick her left. "So did you."

But because Dinah had given Nick the wrong hand, they didn't end up shaking hands, really, as much as holding hands. Nick didn't let go of her hand, and Dinah didn't feel like yanking it away.

"Listen, you two," Mr. Dixon said. "I'm going to be starting a debate team next fall here at JFK, and I want both of you on it, as partners."

It was practically like having a Hollywood talent scout arrive on the scene, movie contract in hand.

"As partners?" Dinah asked.

"You mean, debating on the same side?" Nick asked.

"Yeah," Mr. Dixon said. "Think about it."

The idea was too much for Dinah. She wriggled her hand free of Nick's and hurried down the hallway to seventh-period home ec.

15

After school, Suzanne went with Dinah to Mrs. Briscoe's house to hear Dinah's reenactment of the debate. Mrs. Briscoe served the girls tea and lemon bars, and then Dinah acted out the debate, taking each role in turn. She did such a good job staging Nick's speech that she felt herself becoming convinced by it all over again. Her own speech and rebuttals sounded even better the second time around, so that she almost—but not quite—convinced herself back again. Then, in her best gruff Dixon voice, she announced the class vote: fifteen to thirteen.

"So you won!" Suzanne said.

"Not really. It was practically a tie, and it's Mr. Dixon's vote that counts, anyway. And he said"—Dinah switched back to her gruff voice—"I'd have to give it a draw. Class, what you have just heard was a *debate*."

"It was, indeed," Mrs. Briscoe agreed.

"*And* he's starting a debate team next year, and he wants me and Nick to join the team and be partners."

"Partners," Suzanne said meaningfully.

"Not that kind of partner," Dinah said. "Just . . . partners."

Mrs. Briscoe poured Dinah more tea, and Dinah gulped it down.

"Were you and Mr. Briscoe ever in a debate?" Dinah asked then.

Mrs. Briscoe shook her head.

"Or—like, a contest? Where you competed against each other?"

Mrs. Briscoe thought for a bit. She closed her eyes, maybe the better to look far away into the past.

"Yes," she said. "Dinah, talking to you I remember things that I thought were gone forever. Yes, we certainly did, and I came close to not marrying Eddie because of it. When I was young, oh, twenty or so, my passion was anagrams—where you take one word or phrase and rearrange the letters in it to make a new one. I was a bookish sort of girl, and in fact I used to sit and read the dictionary sometimes, just for fun. My favorite pages were the *ob* words. Obsequious. Obstreperous. Obtuse. Obsolescent. So I was a whiz at anagrams, let me tell you. I just knew more words than other people did, and anagrams is all about words.

"Now, Eddie and I had been going together for some time, but we had never played anagrams together. Eddie said he wasn't much for games. Then came the Talents for God night at our church. Each person was supposed to use his or her talent to raise money for the new church organ. So if your talent was baking, you'd sell cookies; if singing, you'd sit at the piano and favor the crowd with some popular tunes."

Dinah wished there would be a Talents for God night at her church. She could raise money by acting *and* debating *and* reciting long poems.

"My talent was anagrams," Mrs. Briscoe went on, "so I set up a challenge, that I'd beat all comers at a dollar a game. I beat seventeen people in a row, too, and then Eddie, who'd been watching the last few games, put a dollar down on the table in front of me. 'I guess I'm ready to give your game a go,' he said."

"Was this before or after the red corn?" Dinah interrupted to ask.

"After. He had gotten to the point where he wasn't afraid to kiss me, and we both pretty much expected we'd get married in the spring. So he plunked that dollar down in front of me, and then he plunked himself down in the challenger's chair, and—girls, it shames me to have to admit it, but he beat me. There went my seventeen-game winning streak, and all the good feeling I'd had about myself as a word champ."

"Were you mad at Mr. Briscoe?" Suzanne asked.

"Mad? Mad wasn't the half of it. I broke off our engagement right then and there. I told him that if he was such a fancy anagrams player, I was sure he could find himself another girl to play anagrams with. It sounds petty and ridiculous now, but my pride was hurt, to be beaten like that by my own fellow in front of half the congregation. I didn't speak to Eddie for days."

"And then what happened?" Dinah asked.

"Then my birthday came around, and Eddie came by my house with some violets and a little white envelope, and in the envelope was a note that just said 'A Violet Time.' Well, I could see right away that 'A Violet Time' was an anagram on 'I Love Mattie.' Mattie is my Christian name."

"And you got married and lived happily ever after," Suzanne concluded.

Mrs. Briscoe nodded. "We did."

"Did you ever play anagrams again?" Dinah asked. "With Mr. Briscoe?"

"Just about every day." Mrs. Briscoe chuckled. "We played anagrams, and we worked the crossword, and when Scrabble came out after the war, we both became fiends for Scrabble. Sometimes Eddie won, and sometimes I did, and it got so it didn't matter which of us had the high score. We so loved playing Scrabble together."

It sounded like Dinah and Nick, debating together. Dinah knew that Nick felt about debating with her the same way she felt about debating with him. The debate had been the most wonderful thing that had happened to her in sixth grade, maybe in her whole life. And it wouldn't have been a hundredth as wonderful if she had debated anyone other than Nick.

Artie? Jason? Todd? It was Nick Dinah wanted to debate, and only Nick. And it was Nick she wanted to be in plays with. And to have hose fights with. And to tease and be teased by. And . . . to go to dances with.

"Did you—" Dinah wasn't sure how to ask the

question. "Was there ever a dance where girls had to ask boys, and you kept not asking Mr. Briscoe, and then you kind of changed your mind, and, well you did? Ask him?"

Mrs. Briscoe patted Dinah's hand. "No. But I know there isn't a human heart that doesn't sometimes tie itself in pretzels, not knowing what it wants."

"It's too late to ask Nick to the dance, anyway," Dinah said.

"No, it isn't," Suzanne said.

"I told everybody I wouldn't. If I asked him, it would be like taking back everything I said."

"I've found in life that the more you say, generally the more you have to take back later," Mrs. Briscoe said gently.

"Dinah Seabrooke isn't the type of girl to like boys," Dinah insisted. For some reason, she was close to tears.

"Dinah, Dinah." Mrs. Briscoe took Dinah's face in her two hands. "People don't come in types. Dinah isn't any *type* of person at all. Dinah is whoever you are. And as you change, Dinah changes, too. And let's hope you do change, that we all change. The only folks who don't change are the ones in Oak Lawn Cemetery."

Dinah felt the hard knot of stubbornness inside her dissolve into hope. She could ask Nick to the dance, if she wanted. She would still be Dinah, either way. Her biographers would have to wait before issuing their blockbuster best-seller: *Dinah Seabrooke, Spinster Girl.* For Dinah's story wasn't written yet. It would take the rest of Dinah's whole life to write it, and no one might be more surprised at the twists and turns of her story than she, Dinah, herself.

"So this is our last day," Mrs. Bevens told Dinah when she arrived at the broadcasting room the next morning. "Here's Friday's list. It's a long one."

Dinah read it over, then fished in her pocket for the folded scrap of paper on which she had written her own little extra morning announcement late the night before. She had learned from her experience with the Pledge of Allegiance that it would be a good idea to have it handy to look at when the time came to read it. Already the thought of it made Dinah's pulse throb in her temples.

"This is your chance to show us all how slowly you've learned to speak," Mrs. Bevens said.

"I . . . will . . . set . . . a . . . world . . . record . . . for . . . slow . . . speaking," Dinah said.

Mrs. Bevens laughed, but Dinah felt too nervous to laugh along with her.

Three minutes to eight. Two minutes. One.

The first bell. The second bell.

"Please rise and salute the flag."

Somehow Dinah plowed her way through the announcements. She could feel herself reading too fast even without looking for Mrs. Bevens's warning signal. Then, avoiding any telltale pause, she turned to her own handwritten addition to the typed list of announcements for Friday morning, May 10, at JFK Middle School.

136

"D. S., also known as O. R., sometimes also F. H., would like to invite N. T. to the sixth-grade S. H."

Dinah glanced at Mrs. Bevens, but her teacher was concentrating on the speed of the announcements, not their content. She motioned Dinah to slow down.

"This is Dinah Seabrooke," Dinah read in a final burst. "Have a good day."

"Oh, Dinah, dear, I'm afraid you ended on a rather, well, rapid note," Mrs. Bevens said as she clicked off the microphone. "But overall you did very nicely this week, and there's always next year for you to slow down a bit."

In the hallway outside the front office, the enormity of what Dinah had just done overcame her. Had anybody heard her invitation? Had everybody heard her invitation?

Had Nick heard her invitation?

She couldn't go to English class and face him there, face him and the rest of her classmates. She would have to spend the period in the nurse's office, lying down on one of the little white cots hidden behind the privacy screen.

Suddenly Blaine was beside her. "You sure read the announcements fast this morning, Dinah," she said.

Blaine didn't say anything about Dinah's last announcement. Maybe the public address system had miraculously failed at the crucial moment. Or maybe Dinah had only imagined reading the extra announcement. Maybe she hadn't actually read it at all.

"Come on, Dinah," Blaine said. "You'll be late to class."

Dinah fell in step beside her, more relieved than she could say.

"I didn't quite catch one announcement," Blaine went on. "At the end? It had a bunch of initials in it."

Dinah's heart pounded. She made herself shrug. "I just read whatever they gave me."

Once they reached Mr. Prensky's room, Dinah went directly to her seat without letting her eyes roam the room for Nick. She didn't even want to talk to Suzanne, but Suzanne reached over and squeezed her hand.

"You did it!" Suzanne said. And Dinah knew that Suzanne didn't mean that she had set a schoolwide record for rapid-fire reading of morning announcements.

"O. R.!" Dinah heard from the back of the room. But she didn't turn around. "F. H.! D. O. R., I'm talking to you!"

The bell rang as a paper airplane launched somewhere at the rear of the room came to a graceful landing on Dinah's desk.

Dinah ignored it.

"Do you want me to read it for you?" Suzanne asked.

Dinah didn't answer.

Then she let herself glance down at it. In bold letters on the folded paper, like the airplane's insignia, she couldn't help but read Nick's answer.

Y. E. S.

16

"What time do you want me to drive you to school for the dance?" Dinah's father asked her at dinner.

"Um . . . Well, actually, I don't need a ride," Dinah said. "I sort of asked a boy to the dance, after all, and his father is driving us. They'll be here at a quarter to eight."

"Which boy?" Dinah's mother asked, surprised.

There was no way she could not tell them.

"Nick," Dinah confessed.

"Nick!" Dinah's father exclaimed.

"Nick!" Dinah's mother echoed.

"Nick! Nick! Nick! Nick!" Benjamin banged on his high-chair tray with his two chubby, sticky fists.

"Nick," Dinah replied.

So that was that. One good thing about Dinah's parents was that they didn't say, I thought you hated Nick, or But didn't you say you wouldn't invite Nick in a million billion years? or My, my! *Somebody* changed her mind. Maybe they knew that people changed their minds, and themselves, all the time.

Suzanne was wearing a skirt and blouse to the dance, so after dinner Dinah changed into a skirt and blouse, too. She tried on her orange socks, and she tried on her pink socks, and she tried on a pair of blue-and-white striped socks. In the end she decided to wear one orange sock and one pink one, the way she had planned at the beginning.

At a quarter to eight, the doorbell rang. This time when Dinah opened the door, Nick wasn't hiding in the bushes. He was standing in front of her, pale and polite, wearing good pants and a dress shirt and an orange-and-pink polka-dot bow tie.

"We match," he said, pointing to Dinah's socks.

"We do," Dinah said, in a voice that came out too high and squeaky, not at all like her low, businesslike, morning-announcements voice. But you didn't have to marry someone just because his bow tie matched your socks.

Dinah's parents introduced themselves to Nick and complimented him on his bow tie. Then Dinah followed Nick to the car.

"Good evening, Dinah," Mr. Tribble said. "Don't you look pretty!"

The rest of the ride was strangely quiet. Neither Nick nor Dinah said a word all the way to the school. Once they reached the gym, Dinah hurried off to join her friends in the girls' group, while Nick joined the awkward clump of boys standing beneath the opposite basketball hoop, as far away from the girls as physically possible.

A few minutes later, Mr. Roemer stepped to the microphone and welcomed them all to their first school dance. "This dance is a special one," Mr. Roemer said. "All profits from the ticket sales are going to be donated to our new schoolwide recycling program. And for that we have to thank two dedicated and hard-working sixth graders: Blaine Yarborough and Dinah Seabrooke."

The others clapped, the girls on one side of the gym, the boys on the other.

Then the first song began to play, a fast song. No one danced. No one moved.

"The first dance," Mr. Roemer announced over the sound of the music, "is a boys' choice. Boys, it's up to you now."

One by one, slowly, reluctantly, individual boys began to break away from the group and edge their way across the vast middle of the gym to approach the girls.

Nick came up to Dinah. "May I have the pleasure?" he asked, with a bow. Dinah made a curtsy, and they danced. Just like that. It wasn't too bad, really, dancing with a boy to a fast song. It was even fun, when the boy was Nick.

For the next song, Dinah danced with Greg Thomas, Suzanne's boyfriend, and the song after that she danced with Blaine's date, Amory Cruz. Then an unmistakably slow song came on.

"Dinah?"

Nick was there, holding out his hand.

"I don't really know how to dance," Dinah said, stalling for time.

"Neither do I," Nick said.

Dinah let Nick put one hand in the middle of her back. She put her left hand on his shoulder and held his other hand with her right. Cautiously, shyly, they moved back and forth in time to the music. It turned out that dancing wasn't a thing you had to know how to do. It was something you just did. And slow-dancing with a boy you liked was every bit as wonderful as dancing on a rooftop in the rain.

Dinah danced with Nick three more times, and then they drifted over to the refreshment table for punch and pretzels.

"Are you going to sign up for the debate team next year?" she asked.

"Uh-huh. Are you?"

Dinah nodded.

"About the capital punishment debate—" they both began at the same time.

"You first," Nick said.

"No, you first," Dinah said.

"Well, do you want to have, like, our own debate again sometime?" Nick asked. "I thought of a couple more arguments I didn't use in class."

Dinah's words came in a rush. "How about, this time you argue *for* capital punishment and *I'll* argue against. Because you know what? I think I don't believe in capital punishment anymore. I stopped believing in it halfway through the debate."

"You're on," Nick said. "When do you want to do it?"

Dinah looked around the gym. A fast song was playing. Fast songs weren't her favorite.

"Like now?"

"Why not?"

Nick led Dinah toward the bleachers. Then, halfway there, he stopped suddenly and whirled around and kissed her, the way Todd had done when they'd practiced the closing scene from *Love Saves the Day*. But this time it was a real kiss, not a playacting kiss.

"There!" Nick said. "See, I don't always burp when I want to kiss someone."

Could one week really have had in it morning announcements, the debate, a dance, and a kiss?

They reached the bleachers and climbed together to the quietest corner.

"You thought we had a debate last time, Ocean-River? Your doom awaits you!"

Then Nick looked worried. "Can I still call you Ocean-River? Now that I've kissed you?"

"What else would you call me?"

"How about 'dearest Ocean-River'? Or 'Frizz Head, my love'?"

"My hair isn't frizzy, it's curly," Dinah said.

And they sat on the bleachers, hand in hand, ready for the next debate.